"Warning needed: whatever you do—
just buy the book! Do not try to read parts in
a public place! This one is seriously, seriously
passionately hot! An absolute sizzler!"
—*FreshFiction.com* on *SHAMELESS*

"Tori Carrington's imagination knows no boundaries
and she proves it once again."
—*Romance Reviews Today* on *UNBRIDLED*

"Filled with passion, angst, and a very interesting
relationship between two strong people,
this novel is hot, hot, hot!"
—*The Romance Readers Connection* on *BRANDED*

"Get out the asbestos gloves to read this one,
it's almost too hot to handle."
—*Writers Unlimited* on *RECKLESS*

"Consistently excellent authors
with surprising emotional depth."
—*The Romance Readers Connection* on *RECKLESS*

"One of category's most talented authors."
—*EscapetoRomance.com*

Blaze

Dear Reader,

Take one part bad girl on the run, one part alpha male determined to catch her, add a healthy helping of sexual chemistry and physical danger and you have the makings of this latest Tori Carrington title!

In *Guilty Pleasures,* former Army Ranger Jonathon Reece is determined to make a name for himself in his new career with private security firm Lazarus, but he has his work cut out for him on his first big solo assignment: bringing in fugitive-from-justice Mara Findlay. The problem? The sexy bad girl outwits him at every turn.

Mara is innocent of the crime of which she's accused, but why bother explaining that? Instead, she's going to prove it. Problem? The hottie on her heels.

Sex is just sex, isn't it? Not when it's the kind you can't get enough of. And when circumstances allow for both time and opportunity, Mara and Jon take full advantage…until it's not about just the sex anymore. But during a time when nothing is as it appears, can Mara and Jon trust each other? More important, can they trust what they're feeling is real?

We hope you enjoy Jon and Mara's sizzling, heart-thumping journey toward sexily-ever-after. Curious about upcoming Tori titles? Visit www.facebook.com/toricarrington.

Here's wishing you love, romance and HOT reading.

Lori Schlachter Karayianni & Tony Karayianni
a.k.a. Tori Carrington

Tori Carrington

GUILTY PLEASURES

HARLEQUIN®
entertain, enrich, inspire™

Recycling programs
for this product may
not exist in your area.

ISBN-13: 978-0-373-79707-3

GUILTY PLEASURES

ABOUT THE AUTHOR

RT Book Reviews Career Achievement Award-winning, bestselling duo Lori and Tony Karayianni are the power behind the pen name Tori Carrington. Their more than fifty novels include numerous Harlequin Blaze miniseries, as well as the ongoing Sofie Metropolis, PI comedic mystery series with another publisher. Visit www.toricarrington.net and www.sofiemetro.com for more information on the couple and their titles.

Books by Tori Carrington

This book is dedicated to fellow readers
who like their stories hot and dangerous!
And, as always, to editor extraordinaire Brenda Chin,
who always gets it....

1

JONATHON REECE READ the detailed stat sheet, giving the grainy photos of an attractive brunette in the corner a cursory glance: the one on the right appeared to be a high school senior yearbook shot of Mara Findlay showing a clean-cut girl every guy in class likely panted over; the other was a mug shot of a woman with spiky blond hair and raccoon eyes, more wild animal than girl next door. The two were polar opposites, appearing to have no more connection to one another than a kitten did to a bobcat. He'd known his share of both, drawn more to the former than the latter.

Although this was the first time he was asked to hunt either down.

He looked across the desk at his boss, Darius Folsom.

"You up for it?" Darius asked.

Was he up for it? He'd been waiting for just such a solo assignment, to prove to his higher-ups that he was Lazarus Security material, not just capable in an ensemble assignment, but on his own, as well. And this, essentially a high-profile bounty hunter case, was right up his alley. Given his army ranger background, he knew he'd get his man—or in this case, woman—before any of the federal or local agencies, not to mention other bounty hunters. And he'd do it quick and be first in line for the next job.

"All over it," he said with a grin.

Darius got up from his chair and rounded the desk. "Good. You've got contact info should you need backup. Don't hesitate to use it."

"I won't." Only he didn't plan on needing any assistance. This was a clear-cut assignment. He had this.

Jon shook Darius's hand, and thanked him, then traded the stark office for the long corridor leading to the back entrance.

Lazarus Security was a newer operation, but already they were creating a name for themselves in the private sector, attracting high-profile cases and consistently delivering the goods. Not that Jonathon was surprised. Before he'd signed on, he'd heard of the five partners who, although not much older than him, were gaining mythical status within the military and personal security communities. Each had earned their stripes individually, but it was their combined story that guaranteed that whenever soldiers were gathered, active or veteran, it would be told.

He nodded at a new recruit, even as he took his cell phone out to make arrangements with Lazarus's go-to gal to catch the first flight out to Arizona.

The fact that Winslow was also his hometown was a bonus. He knew Arizona as well as he knew where the dust on the tops of his boots came from. He gave in to a small grin as he exited the building and climbed inside his old Jeep Wrangler, his gaze catching momentarily on the top-of-the-line shooting range and the new recruits being trained there by Megan McGowan.

He was really here, wasn't he?

Yes, he was.

And he intended to not only stay here, but become worthy of partner status in record time.

He started the Jeep, running down what he needed to do in his mind. He'd stop by the small rental house he'd just moved into with his girlfriend, Julie, grab the duffel he'd kept packed ever since becoming a ranger and then head to the airport.

Miss Mara Lynn Findlay didn't stand a chance....

THERE WASN'T A CHANCE in hell anyone would expect her to make an appearance back at her place....

Mara Findlay gave her recently dyed brassy red hair a tousle so bangs fell over her green eyes and nudged her way past two slow moving passengers as she walked through Phoenix's Sky Harbor Airport gate entrance into the terminal, her destination a long-term parking lot where she always kept a car. An old Chevy with no electronics that could be traced, much less lead, back to her.

The scent of freshly brewed coffee teased her and she stared hungrily at a small diner as she passed.

She'd been running nonstop for over two days and there was so much caffeine already in her system, she fairly vibrated. To add more to it would be nothing short of stupid. As soon as she did what she needed to do back at her warehouse apartment, she'd better find a place to get some solid sleep if she hoped to keep her wits about her.

And, oh, boy, did she ever need to keep her wits about her....

Well, here's another nice mess you've gotten me into.

The Laurel and Hardy quote her father had been fond of usually made her smile, but it didn't now. Very few things were capable of making her smile right about then. Being wanted for murder tended to have that effect on a girl.

She hurried through the airport terminal, chin ducked down as she felt her way through her backpack for an energy bar.

She smacked headfirst into someone emerging from another arrival gate.

"Criminy, they put eyes in your head for a reason," she mumbled, crouching to pick up the bar that had fallen to the floor.

"Most probably so they could be poked out by the likes of someone like you," a man said.

She got the bar and began walking before she was even upright.

"Why, thank you for the reminder of why I'm still single," the man said.

Mara couldn't help herself. She smiled. She spared the guy a look and wasn't disappointed by what she saw—tall, dark and sarcastic. Just her type.

While no one would describe her as short, this guy had her by at least five inches and was long and lean, somewhere around her age, and boasted blond surfer-dude good looks that normally might have repelled her but somehow didn't, in his case. Mainly because, while he might look like a surfer, she'd bet he didn't own a board and he probably only went into the water to swim for fitness, so his brain wasn't waterlogged and limited to the words *awesome* and *dude*.

No, this guy had military—or ex-military—stamped all over him.

Too bad she was in such a hurry. She might have considered talking him into taking her back to his place, giving him a nice, long ride, then crashing for ten hours straight before hitting the ground running again.

Of course, despite his comment, he was probably as single as a two-dollar bill.

She gave him a two-finger salute and watched him first look at his cell phone, then return a half-assed smile that told her she was probably missing out on a primo op for some great sex.

Ah, well. Story of her life. Fantasy was always much more interesting than reality, in her world. In her mind, she slept with any number of hot guys a day. In reality, you could count the number of men with whom she'd ever been intimate on one hand without the use of the thumb.

She emerged from the airport terminal and blinked against the hot, bright Arizona sunlight. She'd forgotten for a moment where she was. Which told her her need for sleep was greater than she'd realized. Maybe she should grab that rest before going back to her place, just in case it was being watched.

But what she needed couldn't wait.

Damn.

She boarded a shuttle to an off-site long-term parking lot right before it closed its doors, standing instead of sitting, and watched the guy she'd run into come outside the terminal, shielding his eyes. Their gazes met and held until broken by distance, as the hum of the shuttle engine filled her ears.

In a parallel universe, she might have found herself straddled across his bare thighs at that moment, riding him through long, mountainous trails toward an awesome waterfall...

She grimaced.

In a parallel universe, she wouldn't be wanted for the murder of a man whose only crime was to be assigned to hear a capital case against a militia head who had no intention of staying in jail.

She absently rubbed her forehead. She still wasn't clear on everything that had happened, other than what she'd read in the papers. Federal Prosecutor Ryan Mussel had been killed in his home office...and apparently there had to have been enough trumped-up evidence left around to link his murder to her, since she had an outstanding arrest warrant.

Her step faltered.

While she hadn't known Ryan personally, she had known about him and had seen him on a couple of occasions years ago. She certainly had no motive for his murder. But she could only imagine what evidence had been manufactured against her: enough to earn her at least a life sentence if not a death one.

But why? What did she know? There had to be a reason she was being set up for a crime she hadn't committed. By a man she had once loved, along with his extended family. A family that had also been *her* family not so very long ago, although it sometimes seemed like a lifetime had passed since she'd left the Freedom Way militia group to which she'd once belonged.

"No one ever truly gets out…."

She recalled the words of one of her "family" members when she'd said goodbye to him.

"Once in, you're always in. And not always in a good way."

She hadn't completely grasped what he'd been saying…until now.

She could only hope the information she was after would be enough to clear her name.

Of course, getting that information was going to be tricky.

Tricky? To most, it would represent a death wish.

But seeing as she was probably facing the death penalty anyway...well, she had to risk it.

First she had to get what she needed from her place, the most important thing being cash.

She tightened her grasp on the pole as the shuttle turned a corner, suddenly cold despite the high heat....

JON'S CELL CHIMED several times the instant he switched it on, once the plane had parked at the arrival gate. Every time it did, he checked to watch another text roll in from Julie. Twelve of them at last count. He didn't kid himself into thinking they would be the last. He could only wonder when the calls would start.

Scratch that; they already had. Three voice mails were waiting for him.

He didn't need to check. He already knew what he'd hear. Maybe not Julie's exact words, but the gist of those words. Essentially, he was a low-down dirty heel for leaving her high and dry with no warning. What was she going to do by herself for God knows how long? They were supposed to meet her parents for dinner. He couldn't possibly expect her to go by herself?

The messages weren't anything that couldn't wait until later, when he had both the time and the patience to listen to her rant.

He stood outside the terminal doors staring at the woman he'd run into in the terminal. She looked back at him. As was the case inside, he felt an odd prickling at the back of his neck.

He absently rubbed the area in question and then

checked his cell phone again, which was exactly what he'd been doing when he'd bumped headlong into the hot redhead.

Only, *hot* didn't begin to cover it. He'd experienced an immediate physical awareness when her body had brushed against his. Only, she'd regained her bearings and then continued walking without missing a musical beat, issuing the verbal comment as easily as if she'd been wishing him a good day. Talk about one-sided attraction....

He squinted at the shuttle as it disappeared, leaving nothing behind but an invisible cloud of diesel fumes and a lingering sensation that he was missing something. But that didn't make sense. He and Julie had just moved in together, their relationship going on two years, and he'd never once been tempted to stray. Despite her occasional—okay, maybe more like frequent—temperamental rants, their relationship was solid.

He grimaced. Okay. Maybe it wasn't all that rock-hard. He'd suspected, their first day together under the same roof, that he'd made a mistake. He'd hoped things would get better. But in the two months since the day, he'd found himself spending more time at work than at home. Which, of course, aggravated her all the more—

"Mr. Reece?" He heard his name above the sounds of shuttle engines and airplane traffic.

He spotted a pimply kid who looked barely old enough to drive standing next to a beat-up old Jeep.

"That would be me," he said.

"Your car, sir."

He'd specifically asked for a rental from a used car lot, as opposed to one of the national agencies, preferring something tried and true, without an identifying sticker on a cookie-cutter sedan that would immediately identify him as an out-of-towner—something he was not, despite now living in Colorado Springs.

Speaking of which, he hoped he'd be able to squeeze in some time to see his family, maybe after he delivered one very wanted Mara Lynn Findlay to the sheriff. He knew his mom wouldn't mind him popping up on her doorstep unannounced. And any one of his four siblings would enjoy a visit. If everything went the way he hoped, he might finish up in time to have dinner at his mom's, and a beer with one or three of his brothers and his sister at Flossie's Tavern. Then he could soon be on a plane home, in time to have a long-overdue talk with Julie about the volatility of their relationship.

Yes. Sounded like a plan.

Jon opened the Jeep's passenger door, stashed his duffel inside, then closed and locked it. He took the key from the kid and then handed him a twenty.

"Thanks."

He rounded the Jeep and climbed in the driver's side. He put the vehicle in gear and pulled away, his destination the apartment of one particular fugitive from justice, Mara Lynn Findlay....

2

JON WAS UNSURPRISED to find that Mara's place wasn't so much an apartment as it was space above an abandoned warehouse. He was familiar with the district. Jancy's was an old automotive tool-and-die operation that finally closed its doors at some point in the mid-'90s. His uncle had spent a lifetime working there, as had a couple of cousins...until the factory shut down without warning, leaving them high and dry with no more than a Closed sign on the door one morning when they reported to work.

Judging by the large Realtor sign affixed to the brick exterior, it was still standing empty.

Except for the upstairs apartment...

Jon parked the Jeep in the back corner behind an old Dumpster that probably didn't see regular garbage pickup, and got out. There wasn't much traffic in this area outside Winslow. Not now that the few factories that had once kept the town humming had shut down. He was glad he hadn't gone through a car rental agency. A shiny new Ford would look a lot more out of place than his old Jeep.

He looked around at the weed-choked cracked asphalt, piles of discarded tires and empty wooden pallets. On second thought, any kind of vehicle that wasn't a rusty shell and whose engine ran, period, would stand out.

He squinted against the strong midday sun, his black T-shirt and dark jeans absorbing the heat as thirstily as a sponge, his shoulder holster and 9 mm heavy against his skin. If the Feds were anywhere around, they were well hidden. He walked toward the back of the warehouse and the wrought-iron stair-well where a large mailbox sat crammed full of what he guessed was junk mail. The warehouse itself was unremarkable: a long, simple building that was a mix of brick and aluminum sheeting, with windows lining the tops of the walls to allow for natural lighting, and large doors spaced throughout, presumably for shipping purposes. Above the original building was a second story that ran maybe a quarter of the length of the structure itself, probably once housing the factory offices. Now, he guessed it was a personal apartment. He grabbed the railing, about to climb the stairs, when movement through the grimy window to his left caught his attention. He went to the large, double-loading doors and cupped his hands to stare inside.

A Camaro. An old one, whose windshield had recently been cleaned by the wipers.

He automatically drew his gun and tried the door. It opened easily…quietly.

Shit. That couldn't be good.

His thought was verified when he felt something hard hit him on the back of the head. He was aware of the cement floor jumping up to smack him in the face before all went dark….

MARA KICKED THE 9 MM away from the guy's hand, checked to make sure he was out, then gave the area outside a visual sweep to verify he was alone, before closing the door and, this time, locking it.

She knew she should have seen to that before starting to cover the car. He'd never have gotten inside if she had.

Then again, if she'd gotten home ten minutes earlier, she would have had both the car covered and the door locked, completely bypassing her current circumstances.

She hauled a dusty stretch of canvas over the car, then went about the business of dragging the guy to the far corner of the warehouse, kicking a couple of empty energy-drink cans out of her way as she went. Although she was in excellent physical condition, deadweight was deadweight and he had at least fifty pounds, if not more, on her. And while the temperature in the warehouse wasn't as hot as outside, it was still hot. She finally reached the door to her working office, unbolted it then dragged him inside, wiping her damp brow with the short sleeve of her black-and-white T-shirt before sitting him upright and taking a good look at him.

Huh.

He was the guy from the airport.

What were the odds?

She stood straight, twisted her lips and considered him for a long moment. She'd tagged him as ex-military when they'd crossed paths before. But what would he be doing here—alone—now?

She didn't have to think too hard—he'd obviously been sent to apprehend her.

She leaned back, staring at where his 9 mm still lay in the middle of the open old warehouse—now her workshop—floor.

He began to stir.

Damn.

Having nothing on her to use as a restraint, and guessing he did, she was left with only one option, short of knocking him unconscious again.

She leaned forward and kissed him…

SHARP PAIN SHOT THROUGH the back of Jon's head. Where was he?

And who in the hell was kissing him?

He blinked open his eyes, aware of three things: he was sitting on a cold, cement floor. He wasn't there voluntarily. And the woman straddling his hips wasn't his girlfriend.

Boy, if Julie was pissed before…

Especially since he was starting to enjoy the kiss.

He couldn't be sure who she was, but she tasted of chocolate and mint and knew her way around a man's mouth.

Jon groaned, caught between wanting to go with the moment and needing to get a handle on the situation.

Her hands felt around his stomach, dipping down into his waistband, then his rear end. Her tongue lapped at the corners of his lips then slid inside his mouth, teasing his, even as her thighs squeezed him, making him overly aware of how close her pelvis was against his.

She smoothed her hands down over his shoulders, his arms...

Then she was grabbing his wrist, twisting it until he was facedown on the cement, the plastic teeth of a restraint being drawn tight together. In seconds, he found his hands tied behind his back—and around a six-inch metal support pole.

Sweet hell...

The woman rose to her feet even as he sat back upright, staring up at her.

There was no way on earth that she was...

"You," he said simply.

Everything came together at once: the woman running into him at the airport; the stat sheet with the grainy photos; the whack of something solid hitting the back of his head.

He winced. It wasn't possible he'd been taken hostage by his own target. Was it?

"Me," she said.

Jon tested the restraint behind his back, half-afraid it was his own. Which meant the police-grade plastic bracelet would be doubly hard to get out of.

Mara Lynn Findlay wore the same jeans and black-and-white T-shirt she'd had on at the airport, but she'd tied her shiny—and, he highly suspected, dyed—red hair back from her face. She looked nothing like either of the photos on the sheet.

Then again, there had also been nothing listed on that stat sheet that indicated she'd be anything other than an easy grab. Her occupation was listed as "an artist." He hadn't expected her to be as fit and capable as a ranger.

She pointed a short, black-painted fingernail at him. "I'm guessing you know a whole hell of a lot more about me than I know about you," she said. "So why don't we remedy that, shall we?"

"Oh? I'm beginning to think I might not know anywhere near as much as I needed to know about you."

He realized she had his wallet. She flipped it open and stared at his driver's license, counted his money then put it back inside, then counted two credit cards, one issued through Lazarus for business, along with his most recent hunting license.

"Bounty hunter?"

"In a manner of speaking."

"Independent?"

"Associated."

"Out of where?"

"Colorado Springs."

She raised her brows at that and tossed his wallet onto a desktop.

"I just got in a little while ago." He offered up a sarcastic smile. "But of course you know that."

She was watching him closely. "Army...ranger, I'm guessing."

He raised a brow. "Target on."

"Must really piss you off that you're sitting on the floor of my warehouse in your own restraints."

"You have no idea."

She moved toward the corner of what looked like an office, the windows giving a one-hundred-and-eighty-degree view of what had once been a factory floor. He peeled his gaze from her primo behind and looked through the open door. A few of the die machines were still in place, dusty and dry. He made out the now covered Camaro and just beyond that, his gun.

He winced again.

Oh, this was so not going anywhere on his trip report.

He also saw that her art medium of choice seemed to be metal sculptures.

Positioned around the open area closest to them were at least three of what he'd guess were works in progress, one of them towering nearly to the warehouse ceiling and resembling a robotlike Greek statue, the others considerably shorter, perhaps too new to show what they'd ultimately end up representing. Two thigh-high piles of scrap metal lay just on the other side of them. Welder's gear of full mask, goggles and gloves were nearby, along with an industrial-size blowtorch as well as a smaller one.

He glanced back at her, easily imagining her wearing the full mask and working with red-hot fire.

"How about you?" he asked.

"Me, what?" She rifled through drawers looking for something.

"Ex-military?"

She hesitated. "No."

He guessed that wasn't entirely true. But surely, information of that nature would have been listed on her sheet. Going after a soft-around-the-middle civilian was a much different job than pitting wits against someone with the same training.

He allowed his gaze to take her in, from her toned arms, her full breasts, flat abs and an ass you could probably bounce a quarter off. Military or not, she'd obviously had training. And not of the fluffy Zumba variety, either. The fact that she had gotten one over on him was evidence of that.

Again, it was something that should have been on her stat sheet.

Mara appeared exasperated as she slammed shut the drawer of a metal desk then propped her hands on her hips. She looked toward the areas that allowed a view outside.

"You alone?" she asked.

"You expect me to answer that?"

She smiled, reminding him of a predatory creature capable of taking a bite out of him. More like the bobcat he'd compared her to when he'd first seen her photos.

The fact that the idea excited him? Probably should have been of greater concern than it was.

His cell phone rang, the chime "MMMBop" by Hanson chosen by Julie herself.

Damn.

Mara stared at him, then at his front jeans pocket. "Someone important?"

"No."

She leaned forward and fished the phone out. "Julie? With a heart? Looks important to me."

He didn't say anything. For reasons he preferred not to delve into just then, he just hoped she wouldn't answer it.

She didn't.

He let out the breath he was holding.

Her amused expression told him she'd caught his reaction. "I think you're lying to me." She waved the cell at him. "How do you suppose Miss Julie-with-a-Heart would feel about your kissing another girl?"

"I don't have to suppose. It would piss her off."

She smiled then tossed the phone to the desk to lie next to his wallet. "I figure I have another five minutes, tops, before you break that restraint," she said. "Which means I've got two minutes to get something else. Be right back."

He watched her leave the office and climb a set of dark, steel stairs to a catwalk he guessed must lead to her upstairs apartment.

Damn.

She was right. It would take him at least another few minutes to free himself.

She was back in one.

She planted one of the old boots she wore between his legs, nudged his knees farther apart and then moved what he guessed was a steel toe closer to his family jewels than he was comfortable with. She leaned over so she could secure the pair of police-issue steel handcuffs she'd brought down.

Aw, hell.

As irritated as he was growing, he couldn't help but peer down the front of her shirt as she worked, her breasts swaying ever so slightly in a shiny, black bra, a thin, glistening sheen of sweat on her smooth skin from her recent efforts. She smelled of something sweet and sexy that made his mouth water in a way that would only further piss off "Julie-with-a-Heart."

What was he talking about? It was pissing him off. The last thing he wanted was to feel attracted to a woman who had taken him hostage when he was supposed to be hauling her in instead.

She finished then stepped back, taking what appeared to be a toaster pastry from where she'd been holding it between her lips and chewing silently. She held it out toward him. "Bite?"

"What are you planning to do?" he asked, ignoring her question.

"Now? In the immediate future?" She waved the pastry. "Eat this."

He had to admit, she wasn't boring.

Although he'd much prefer it if their roles were reversed.

"And after that?"

Her chewing slowed and she used a pinkie to swipe a crumb from the corner of her mouth. "Sleep."

Sleep...

The word wound around his mind even as he watched her toe a bedroll she'd brought down along with the restraints and what appeared to be documents of some sort folded and stashed in a small, blue plastic bag he sometimes saw newspapers delivered in. She popped the last of the pastry into her mouth and opened the sleeping bag, stuffing the documents inside before stretching out on top of it. It was only then he recognized the signs of fatigue: the dark smudges under her green eyes, the paleness of her skin, the lethargic lag of her movements.

Hell, if this was what she was like at half speed, he'd hate to see her at full.

She'd positioned the bedroll so it was far enough away that he couldn't reach her, but between him and the door, close enough that if he awkwardly tried to escape, he'd have to step over her.

He eyed the open door.

She looked up abruptly then reached to slam the door. There was no mistaking the auto lock that clicked home.

Swell.

"How long you plan to be out?" he asked.

"As long as my body dictates. Try anything stupid and…"

He hadn't realized she'd brought a gun down with her.

Oh, wait: she hadn't. That was his gun.

Damn.

It was going to take him a while to live down this one. Not that he planned on telling anyone. No. But it *was* going to take a while for *him* to get over this.

The sound of her soft snores a moment later told him she was out like a light.

Jon drew in a deep breath and felt around his own restraints.

The way he saw it, all he had to do was wait until she decided what to do next before he figured out his next move.

He could only hope that hers didn't include putting the muzzle of his own gun to his head and shooting, much the way she had assassinated the good prosecutor she was wanted for murdering.…

3

"I'M HENRY THE EIGHTH."

Mara fought against the irritating words determined to yank her from a solid sleep.

He sang the words louder, apparently convinced she hadn't heard him the first time.

She put her hands over her ears and moaned.

No, no, no…

"Oh, hi," her annoying hostage said. "Sorry…am I bothering you?"

She cracked open an eyelid and glared at him, noting how close the 9 mm was…and how easy it would be to do away with the annoyance.

"By the way?" he said, his long, denim-covered legs casually crossed at the ankles of his cowboy boots, looking as though he was there by choice and not by force…and appearing a little too cheerful for her liking. "You already know from reading my license, but we haven't been properly introduced. My name is Jonathon Reece, Jon to my friends. But I'll let you call me that if you want…"

She glanced at her watch. She'd only been asleep for a couple of hours. She reached for the gun and dragged it closer to her side.

"I'm thinking it's been a while since you've gotten any decent sleep, huh? Actually, I'm guessing it's been nearly forty hours. You know, the time that prosecutor bit it…"

She squinted at him, sorely tempted to pull the trigger.

"That's a long time to go without rest. It messes with the system, big-time. Throws you off your game."

Groaning aloud, she rolled smoothly to her feet, taking the gun with her.

"Hey, a movie song isn't grounds for execution in most states."

She opened a drawer, looking to grab something she saw in there earlier. "What movie song?"

"The one I was singing. You know, from *Ghost?* Patrick Swayze sang it to get Whoopi Goldberg to help him. Just call me Swayze Crazy. Isn't that how the saying goes?"

"I wouldn't know. Never saw the movie. As for the song, it was written in the early 1900s, and popularized by Herman and the Hermits in the mid-'60s, a long time before the movie in question."

"Wow. You're smart."

The more he talked, the more her trigger finger itched.

She found what she was looking for and made her way back to him.

"Did you learn that in school? That song bit?" he asked.

"No. My father liked to pretend he lived in a time period other than the one he was in. Either that or he was stuck in the wrong time. I don't know which."

"What are you going to—"

She slapped a stretch of duct tape across his sexily infuriating mouth. Then just to be sure, she secured another in the shape of an *X*.

She looked into his eyes, the deep shade of blowtorch-blue, with lashes that were somehow too thick to be on a man, yet were ridiculously attractive.

Damn, but he was hot.

She licked her lips, momentarily recalling how it had felt to have them pressed against his. Her kiss had been a completely diversionary tactic, she told herself. If she revisited the naughty thoughts she'd originally had of him at the airport…well, that was between her and her bedroll.

His expression was altogether too suggestive. Could he be thinking along the same line?

She cleared her throat and sat back on her heels.

"Oh, and there is more to that song," she said. "It goes…" She quoted him the full lyrics. "Just so you'll know the next time you choose to annoy someone."

If she didn't know better, she'd say he was grinning at her through the tape.

She cocked her head, her gaze drawn to his mouth.

She picked up a red sharpie from a nearby tabletop, uncapped it then drew another *X* over the tape.

There. A reminder of what was off-limits.

Trouble was? She was having a hard time not thinking *X* marked the spot.

Yes, he kissed that well.

She gave a mental eye roll, checked his restraints—both still firmly in place—then stretched back across the sleeping bag.

She stared at the grimy windows on the other side of the office.

While her attraction to Reece was purely physical, she needed to remind herself that it was another man who had put her in the position she was in now.

She'd been sixteen, had just lost her father, was living with an emotionally unstable and distant mother... and militia member Gerald Butler had smiled that devastating smile at her, offering her what she thought was everything she'd ever need.

She supposed that had been true...for a time. Two years, to be exact. It had taken her that long to figure out that the group and its ideals weren't any better than the organized government against which they rebelled.

And that the man with whom she'd fallen in love didn't know the true meaning of the word.

Of course, she understood how young she'd been then, emotionally as well as in years. And she was happy to say it had been a good long while since she'd actually thought about that time in her life.

Until now.

Until she'd been plucked out of Butler's files and set up for murder.

Oh, she'd read the news that Gerald had been arrested some time ago for charges that ranged from crimes against the federal government to murder. But she'd barely given the news piece a cursory glance and a heart pang before closing the paper and then lighting her welding torch, returning to her artwork, something that never betrayed her, never lied to her, was always there for her.

If she'd worked for twenty hours straight in order to cleanse thoughts and memories of Butler from her mind before finally collapsing into a dreamless sleep... well, that was between her and the sculpture she'd been working on.

Now, she cleared her throat and rubbed her nose. It was one thing to know someone you loved had never really loved you. Quite another to be set up for murder for reasons she knew benefited him.

"You know, you didn't ask if I did it..." she said quietly to Reece, her body already beginning to succumb to sleep again. "Just saying. If it were me, it would have been the first question I asked."

He didn't respond. Not that he could.

"See you in a while, Reece. Don't try anything stupid..."

HOURS LATER, JON CURSED himself for not keeping a metal handcuff key in the secret pocket sewn inside the waist of his jeans. Then again, he hadn't expected to need one.

He did, however, have a small pocket knife and had long since taken it out and freed himself from the plastic restraints, which were tighter then the metal ones. He'd blindly tried to pick the metal lock with the blade, only to cut himself on the pad of his thumb. He felt the blood drip from his fingers, but knew it wasn't anything serious. It did, however, convince him to stop trying to pick the lock for a while, lest he accidentally hit a vein.

At one point, he'd drifted off to sleep himself, leaning against the metal pole he was tied to. While Mara had switched off the ringer to his phone, she'd left it on Vibrate. And he'd listened as it buzzed almost non-stop where it sat on the desk.

Julie, no doubt.

Damn.

He'd like to say his reaction was because he was afraid she was worried about him. Instead, he was more concerned his cell battery would go dead.

He leaned his head against the pole and cursed.

Julie...

What wasn't there to like? She was blonde, sexy as hell and a kindergarten teacher. All those girl-next-door qualities that brought guys sniffing.

Just when had things started to take a bad turn?

He couldn't really say. They'd dated for two years before moving in together and from the get-go, he'd joked about her control-freak tendencies. He'd found them cute. Sometimes, he'd even enjoyed it when she got grumpy about one thing or another, usually connected with some imagined infraction. And she was adorable. Her sexy pout was the stuff of which dreams were made.

Then he'd left his safe employment as an insurance salesman—a job that bored him all to hell—to take the position with Lazarus....

To say Julie wasn't pleased would be an understatement.

"Come on, honey," he'd pleaded with her for the umpteenth time when he'd left on his first assignment with a Lazarus team to search for a missing girl in Florida. "Just look at this as an opportunity for you to get in some important 'you' time...."

"I don't need 'me' time. I need you," she'd said. "Besides, how am I supposed to get 'me' time when I'm completely responsible for Brutus?"

Brutus was the puggle they'd adopted from an animal shelter. He'd been Jon's surprise to her one Christmas morning.

Oh, she'd been surprised, all right. *Shocked* was more the word. And *unhappy*.

She never let an opportunity pass to pitch a bitch fit. "See, we could take a teacup Chihuahua anywhere we wanted to go. We wouldn't have to worry about imposing on friends," she'd said when he'd arranged a weekend trip to Catalina. "And there would be much less dog dirt to clean up...."

Of course, what had he been thinking? "Julie" time was all the time.

He grimaced.

When had her pouting become irritating?

The phone vibrated again.

Was it him, or did it seem weaker somehow?

Double damn.

Mara's leg jerked.

He glanced at her. She hadn't moved the entire time she'd been asleep. And he was sure she was sleeping. He could tell by her deep, even breathing and soft snores, the latter probably because she'd gone so long without quality shut-eye.

Still, the fact that she could sleep at all, given what was going on, was remarkable in and of itself.

Definitely military.

Or some sort of similar training.

He found his gaze trailing over her, appreciating her form. Where Julie was long-limbed and...well, elegant, Mara was toned and compact. Not that she was short. He guessed the two women were the same height. But where Julie rocked a pair of high-heeled shoes, he guessed Mara would look awkward in them.

And the opposite applied in the case of cowboy boots. At least true ones.

He looked at where Mara still wore her short, black combat boots. Suddenly, he could picture her as a child, the victim of schoolyard teasing: "Your mama wears combat boots."

Likely Mara would have cocked a hand on her hip

and said, "Well, that would make her more capable than yours, now, wouldn't it?"

Julie, on the other hand, would have been horrified at the mere thought.

And so would her Stepford Wife mother.

Jon's gaze traveled up the back of Mara's jeans to where her bottom was rounded and pert, then to the small of her back where her T-shirt had ridden up a bit, revealing a stretch of firm flesh.

He swallowed. Hard.

Which seemed to be the word of the minute, because he found a certain area of his anatomy growing noticeably harder.

He caught sight of a tattoo on the back of her left shoulder where she'd rolled up the sleeve. He squinted, trying to make it out. A bird's wing? Angel? He couldn't tell. There wasn't enough visible.

He heard sound outside.

Jon moved his head so he could see the warehouse interior. The sun slanted low, creating dingy, golden shafts of light against the gritty floor between him and the car some seventy-five feet away. He made out the shape of someone looking in the vehicle-access-door window much the same way he had hours before.

Competition for the bounty?

Made sense.

Then again, the Feds could be making another pass.

The sound of the individual trying the door echoed in the room.

Shit.

He heard the quiet dragging of something metallic across the floor. He realized Mara's breathing was no longer deep and even. She had moved only her arm and was now pulling his 9 mm closer to her side.

Wow…

She slowly turned to look at him, nodding in the direction of the visitor outside the building. "With you?"

He shook his head.

The figure moved from the window. A moment later, Jon made out the sound of quiet footsteps on the stairs leading to her apartment.

Mara was on her feet in a flash, stuffing the blue plastic bag he'd seen her holding earlier inside the front waistband of her jeans and covering it with her shirt, then checking the ammo in the gun: he knew it was a full sixteen rounds. She stuffed that into her waistband, as well.

She stopped to look at him.

For a moment, he suspected she might leave him there. And he could tell she was giving it serious consideration.

Then she said, "If he's not with you, then I can trust you're not going to make any noise, right?"

He gave her a long look.

She yanked the tape from his mouth and then headed for the door.

"The hands?"

She came back, leaned over him much as she had earlier with the same tantalizing view. He heard the teeth give, but when she straightened a moment later, he found his hands were still restrained…only now without the post involved.

She stared at the question on his face. "You won't be needing them. Now up, soldier. I know you know how to move with your hands tied behind your back."

He thought about making a smart-ass comment, but she was already through the door and ripping the tarp from the car.

He got up and began following her, then back-tracked to get his cell and wallet from the desk, stuffing each into back jeans pockets. Then he spotted a click-top pen. Bingo. He palmed it and stuffed it inside the waistband of his jeans before joining her.

She climbed inside the car and reached to open the passenger's door for him. He awkwardly got inside and was trying to figure out a way to close it with his foot when she reached across him, her breasts brushing against his thighs, to close it for him.

Then she reached behind him, taking his cell from his pocket and tossing it to the dash.

He had to give her credit; she didn't miss a trick.

Which made him feel a little less bad about being taken hostage by her.

A little.

"The doors?" he asked.

She gave him a long look. "Blocked from the outside. The bastard parked on the other side."

"Then how are we going to get out—?"

The engine started and the car was in gear before

he could utter the next word. His neck jerked as she sped in Reverse, the old car's monster engine roaring in his ears.

She reached across him and yanked the seat belt across his lap, shoving the latch into his hands behind his back before doing her own.

"Hold on," she said, smiling in his direction.

She pressed a button on the visor. Even as he awkwardly secured his seat belt, he looked over his shoulder, watching as another door, this one a garage type, lifted some fifty yards behind them on the opposite warehouse wall.

"It's not going to make it up in time," he said over the engine's growl.

"It'll make it."

Twenty yards...ten...five...

The top of the car hit the bottom of the door, but it didn't slow them down.

She hit the brakes on the other side and did a one-eighty.

"Oops," she said.

He couldn't help shaking his head, amused.

The car was barely straight before she shoved the stick into Drive, roaring off before the guy in her apartment had any idea what hit him.

Or maybe not.

Jon stared back at a large man in faded, full-out desert military gear rounding the side of the warehouse a hundred yards away. Only, he didn't look like anyone he'd ever served with. This guy had long blond hair tied back and a full beard. And his weapon was Russian, more specifically an AK-47.

Definitely not something an American soldier would be toting.

Militia? Or military-loving mercenary?

That meant their visitors numbered at least two: the one on the stairs and this one.

He caught Mara's glance as she looked away from the same sight. She didn't appear surprised. But if he was expecting any kind of explanation, he was sadly disappointed.

Jon shifted in the seat and worked on getting the click-top pen out of the waistband of his jeans, the spring of which he planned to use to pick his handcuffs....

4

AFTER TEN MINUTES, Mara slowed her speed on the mostly deserted roads for which she'd opted, checking her mirrors every few seconds for signs she'd been followed. She hadn't been.

Or at least it appeared that way.

But it wasn't empty, really, was it? The road behind her was choked with ghosts from her past.

She felt a breath away from having the Pop-Tart she'd eaten this morning hurl from her churning stomach.

Now that the urgency had passed, her worsening circumstances crowded around her, inside her, making it impossible to do much beyond keep the car on the road and stare at the glaring reality of her situation. It wasn't enough that they'd set her up for murder... Now they were trying to kill her.

She checked the road behind her again. Still empty. But she didn't expect it to remain that way.

She passed a slow-moving sedan on the two-lane

highway then screeched to a stop on the right shoulder. Jon looked at her as if she'd gone mad. Which was okay with her; the more unpredictable she came off, the more she had the upper hand.

She'd learned early on that it wasn't curiosity that killed the cat, but predictability. At least when it came to predators. So she made it a point to never do the same thing twice.

Of course, she would have been well served to remember that over the past few years. Instead, she'd allowed herself to be lulled into a false sense of security.

She ignored the horn blow of the sedan as it passed them as she got out of the car and slowly made her way around the vehicle.

Though it had been parked in the off-airport lot for months and, as an older vehicle, had no low-jack tracking device, that didn't necessarily mean it was bug free. And it would certainly explain why she hadn't been followed. If she was being tracked, then there was no need.

It made a tactical kind of sense, their targeting her now. They'd gone through all the trouble of setting her up for the prosecutor's murder. The last thing they needed was for her to be hell-bent on proving her innocence.

If she was surprised and hurt to see an ex–family member standing outside the warehouse toting an AK-47...well, she wasn't about to cop to it.

She did feel a bit of relief that he hadn't taken the

money shot when he'd had the opportunity. But she didn't kid herself into thinking she'd be as lucky next time.

So it wasn't only the local and federal authorities, not to mention who knew what yahoos from private firms—she spared Reece a glance—on her tail. It was also the local militia. People who knew her better than any biological family members, if only because they'd taught her all she knew.

Well, not all. If that was true, she might as well surrender to her fate now.

At any rate, she also understood that it wasn't so much what you knew, but what you did with that knowledge that determined the outcome of any situation.

She only hoped she wasn't as rusty as some of her sculptures back at the warehouse.

She got onto her hands and knees and searched underneath the vehicle, inspecting and prodding all the normal hitch spots along with additional ones. It didn't appear to be wired, but there was no way to be sure. There were too many places and it was too big a vehicle to cover every inch. Besides, technology today was so advanced, a tracker could be the size of a dime and hidden under a floor mat at this point.

Still…

She continued searching under the car, stopping only when she hit a pair of feet standing next to the open passenger's door.

She sat back on her haunches and stared up at Jonathon Reece.

"Remember when you asked why I hadn't asked if you'd done it?"

She squinted.

"My answer is I don't care." He pulled his hands out from behind his back. "Oh, and I'm free...."

He grasped her shoulders, pulled her up then urged her against her own vehicle, fastening her own cuffs on her.

Mara briefly closed her eyes.

Damn. And she'd gotten sleep.

Then she realized maybe that was the problem. She needed caffeine. Massive quantities of it.

"Mind if we stop somewhere for coffee?" she asked as he put her in the passenger's seat and did up her safety belt nice and tight before rolling down her window and closing the door.

He didn't answer until he was buckled into the driver's side. "I'm sure they'll have something you like at the county lockup."

He started the car and did a one-eighty, heading back the way they'd come.

Mara swallowed hard, turning her face into the hot wind coming in through the window.

The car wasn't the only thing that had done a one-eighty. Her mindset had taken a noticeable nosedive since he'd slapped the cuffs back on her.

That was a lie. It had gone south when she'd spotted the gunman back at the warehouse.

Frenemies. Wasn't that a new word spawned recently? Although, what she was in the middle of had nothing to do with petty bickering over who had borrowed what or stolen whose boyfriend: this was a matter of life or death.

Namely, her own.

And then there was Reece....

Ironic that she'd been searching for an enemy presence on her car when it had been right in front of her.

The sun ignited the western horizon, setting the sky on fire. But she barely saw it. Instead, she imagined what waited for her at the other end of their journey.

She'd been running on pure adrenaline since she'd originally returned to her apartment three days ago to find FBI agents waiting for her. She hadn't had a clue what they'd wanted then, but she hadn't been about to stick around to find out. At least not from them. So she'd run. And found out soon enough what she was wanted for.

And understood immediately why.

"Who were those guys back there?"

She blinked to look at Reece.

"At your place. The one guy had *militia* written all over him."

She stared out the window, deciding not to answer him.

What had he said? He hadn't asked if she'd committed the crime for what reason? Oh, yes. Because he didn't care.

He messed around with his cell phone, then cursed

loudly and tried again. She guessed the battery was dead. Not surprising, considering how many times it had vibrated since the moment she'd restrained him back at the warehouse.

She closed her eyes again, feeling sweat beginning to bead between her breasts under her T-shirt.

"You can't turn me over to the local authorities," she said quietly.

He probably hadn't heard her over the roar of the engine and his own rant at his dead cell.

He gave her a long look, proving otherwise. "Oh? Why? Coffee not up to snuff?"

She didn't answer for a long moment, then turned her head where it lay against the backrest, feeling exhaustion saturate her every molecule. It was more than the lack of sleep or even the lull after the adrenaline rush. This was...was...

Antipathy.

Complete and utter disenchantment with the world at large and specifically the people in it.

She'd experienced it only one other time....

She forcibly ousted the memory from her mind and instead focused on the here and now.

Which was looking pretty bleak.

She took a deep breath and told him, "Because you'll be directly responsible for my death if you do, that's why."

Mara wasn't given to drama or exaggeration. She didn't even like saying the words because they sounded too much like both. But in this case, well, the truth was the truth.

"That's for a jury to decide."

She jerked her head to stare at him, feeling her blood warm again. "Trust me, you take me to the sheriff's? I won't ever step inside a courtroom."

The militia was so well connected throughout the local and federal law enforcement communities, not to mention plugged into the electronic highway, period, that the instant her name was entered into any computer, the countdown would begin.

Mara watched as the city limits loomed ahead. The sheriff's office lay on the main drag, five, maybe eight minutes away. Off to the west, the sun was quickly sinking into the sand so the sky to the east was already dark. She yanked on her cuffs. There was nowhere near enough time for her to figure out how to pick them and free herself before they got there. At least not in the mental state she was presently in.

Reece grabbed his cell phone again as if it might have magically recharged itself in the time since he put it down.

"Do you have a phone?" he asked.

Her answer was a stare.

"Yes or no."

"No."

She'd ditched her cell phone on Day One. If the battery was in, it was transmitting, no matter if it was on or off. She'd thought about picking up another one that couldn't be traced back to her, but until she had an actual need for one, what was the use?

He tossed the cell back to the seat between them. "So I'm left to your word."

"Yes."

He slowed the car's speed, but whether it was because he was considering his options or the speed limit had changed, she couldn't say. He was as easy to read as a murky, rain-swollen brook on a stormy day.

When he pulled up in front of the sheriff's office moments later, her heart pitched.

There it was, then.

Damn.

She waited for the will to fight to return, fire up her own personal engine. But everything remained eerily silent.

Did it have something to do with him? Had she been hoping against hope that he'd listen to her? Change his mind? Take her at her word? Trust not only that what she was saying was true, but trust, period?

Who could say? She was so tired. Not only for sleep. She was tired of running on what seemed to be a never-ending treadmill.

With no one to rely on.

It was one thing to know a man you had once loved had set you up for murder.

Another to know he'd also put out a hit on you.

She realized Reece had yet to make a move. She looked to find him staring forward, but not really at the sheriff's office, itself. The engine was still running. His hands were still on the steering wheel. The gear was in Park.

Hope sparked.

Then he looked at her, shut down the engine, pocketed the keys and got out.

"I'll leave the keys with the desk sergeant."

He got out and rounded the front of the car to her side. "Gee, thanks," she said.

He opened her door and helped her out.

He led her toward the curb, grasping on to her wrists behind her back. His hold both touched and angered her in its gentleness and control.

Mara set her back teeth and walked inside when he opened the door.

She supposed she should be fighting him. Fighting this. But while her heart beat an increasingly energizing rhythm, she was waiting for the right time.

"Fugitive turnover," he said to the desk sergeant.

The fortysomething woman behind the counter looked at him then her. "Name?"

He told her.

"I'll be right back."

She disappeared into a windowed office where Mara watched her presumably enter her name into a computer.

"I'd take off the cuffs, but I'm afraid you'll coldcock me."

She stared at Reece, feeling the desire to do just that expand inside her. "You're right to be afraid."

His gaze met hers, communicating…what, exactly? Regret? Triumph? Remorse?

"Sorry, but the name is not coming up. Are you sure you spelled it correctly?" the sergeant said.

Mara raised a brow at Reece.

The two exchanged information again.

The sergeant sighed then shrugged. "Let me go try again…"

She went back into the office.

The unusual activity must have caught the attention of the deputy in the neighboring office. He came out, eyeing Mara and Reece, then disappeared into the other office to talk to the sergeant who was still entering the information, apparently without success.

"Well, well, well… What do you suppose that means?" Mara asked.

Reece's hold had tightened on her wrists. "Computer glitch, I'm sure."

"I'm sure."

They stood quietly while the other two conferred, the deputy picking up the phone.

"Tick tock," Mara said.

Reece looked at her. "What?"

"Nothing. Just starting the countdown clock to when we're no longer alone."

"We're not alone now."

"Oh? Well, I think it's about to get a whole lot more crowded in here quick."

And their new guests would be unwelcome, indeed….

5

REECE HATED TO ADMIT IT, but he was thinking along the exact same lines. This—her name not being in the system, the odd behavior of the two sheriff's employees, the militia-looking guys at her place—rated a blip on his own internal radar.

While a computer error wasn't outside the norm, he was coming to understand that there was nothing normal about this assignment. Which likely explained why a firm like Lazarus was hired on to handle it.

He should have known this job would be anything but straightforward. But he'd allowed himself to be lulled into a false sense of security and faith in his own abilities.

"Look, kid, there are some things in life you're going to have to learn." His father's voice came to him loud and clear. "Number one, never jump into the water unless you know how deep it is. Number two, never jump into the water unless you know how deep it is."

He'd been eight and fishing with his dad in a northern Arizona stream during a camping trip. Something had taken his bait and he'd gone into the water, thinking somehow the action would improve his chances of reeling the fish in. Instead, he'd slipped and found himself being pulled downstream by the fish and the current. He'd taken in a lungful of water and was still grasping on to the pole for dear life when his father yanked him out by his collar and stood him on the bank.

Right now, he was beginning to realize that the water was very deep, indeed.

He glanced at his watch, the two employees still in the office, then at Mara, whose back had gone a little stiffer.

He took out the pen spring he'd pocketed earlier and unlocked her cuffs.

She glanced at him curiously as she rubbed her wrists.

A car's tires screeched out front. They both looked toward the street to find a beat-up red pickup truck pulling up at an angle next to the Camaro.

One of the two men in the front seat was the guy from the warehouse.

Somehow he got the impression they wouldn't be the only ones showing up.

He also didn't think their arrival had anything to do with the communications going on in the office, if only because the deputy had caught sight of the pickup and was reaching for his firearm.

Jon automatically lifted Mara over the counter, where he leapt after her, ducking down even as he slid his gun from his holster. The deputy had dropped the phone and was advancing on the front door and the two heavily armed men wearing camouflage approaching the building outside.

Shit. What in the hell was going on?

He looked at Mara. He didn't know how, but somehow she'd gained possession of a shotgun. Perhaps the sergeant kept one behind the counter for protection. At any rate, she was expertly giving it a once-over, checking to make sure it was armed, then she looked up at him.

In that instant, he knew there wasn't anyone he'd rather have at his side, even if she was the reason he was in this situation in the first place.

"Hey, what in the hell do you think you're doing?" the deputy asked.

Jon peered over the counter to find the deputy holding his gun on the two armed men.

Oh, hell. This was going to be a Charlie Foxtrot and a half. While he was sure there was an armory somewhere in the building, no matter how small, there was no way to reach it between now and the time the first shot was fired. And he was pretty sure that was going to be imminent.

He palmed his gun and prepared to make every shot count…until he felt Mara's hand on his arm.

He looked at her.

She nodded toward the west wall.

He stared down a narrow hallway to see another door there with an exit sign above it. Side access? Escape route?

A split second was all he had.

He indicated for her to precede him. She did, keeping low to the floor but moving faster than some people run. He caught sight of the desk sergeant watching from the other room. He waved to her. Within seconds they were at the metal door, just as the sound of the first bullets were fired....

MARA LED THE WAY OUT, hugging the outside wall until she emerged around the front of the building, then ran flat out for her Camaro. The desk sergeant had run out the back, using her shoulder radio to call for what Mara could only guess was help. Mara held the shotgun at the ready as Reece started up the beast. Once they were both in the car without incident, he tore off, the men only a few feet away so engrossed in shooting at each other they hadn't even noticed Mara's departure until she and Reece were already halfway down the street. Reece made a sharp right-hand turn before they could be targeted with any accuracy.

She had to hand it to him; he thought fast on his feet.

Of course, it would have helped if he'd listened to her from the beginning and never taken her to the sheriff's.

The engine roared and the cooler night air rushed in through the open window, blowing her hair back from her face. She let out a huge sigh of relief when they'd put the town's lights behind them. Now, nothing but desert and a two-lane highway stretched out before them.

She glanced at Reece. His face was set into lines as hard as the metal she worked with, his large hands wrapped around the steering wheel with purpose. Had it really only been a few minutes ago that those same hands had grasped her hips and hoisted her over the counter to protect her? Not that she'd needed it, but the fact that he'd felt compelled to give it without prompting made her skin hum with the desire to feel those hands on her again, another purpose in mind.

Things could have gone down very differently, indeed, had he decided to leave her there and look after himself.

He turned off the road.

She looked around. "What are you doing?"

For a split second, she was half afraid he intended to go back into town.

Instead, he went up the road a bit, stopped at a small gas station that also sold cell phones, and picked up a car charger. He'd left her in the car without a second thought, although he had taken the car keys with him. While it might have been a good idea to make a break for it while he was otherwise occupied, she couldn't think of a safer place for her to be just then. It had been so long since she'd been able to rely on another person. And even if she didn't feel she could completely trust him…well, he'd proved that when the chips were down, he did what was right.

She sat quietly as he plugged the charger into the car, then his cell phone. A little messing around and the thing nearly vibrated out of his hands.

He cursed and tossed the phone to the seat between them before starting the engine and backing out.

"Problems?"

He looked at her for a long moment. "Comparatively? No."

He didn't say anything more. She didn't push.

She'd seen the display when she'd taken the phone from him back at the warehouse. "Julie" with a heart attached had been highlighted. Girlfriend? She'd fathom a yes. She'd also guess that "Julie" had been the one to add the heart. Reece didn't seem like a "heart" kind of guy.

Then again, what did she know? It wouldn't be the first time she was wrong about a guy.

She stared back out the window again, her thoughts traveling to Butler, who had set her up and who, she was sure, had sent the two goons to the sheriff's office.

"I don't think your car is safe," Reece said after they'd been driving awhile.

She'd noticed he'd been making a large rectangle around the city. She'd absently wondered if it was because he still considered going back to the sheriff's office.

"I don't mean mechanically." She noticed the

almost reverent way he touched the dusty dash. "In that regard, she's a gem."

She...

"I think she's been tagged. But I'm not telling you anything you hadn't already suspected. That's what you were looking for when I traded places with you, isn't it?"

She didn't think a response was necessary, so she didn't offer one.

"What are you thinking?" she asked.

"Of trading her for mine."

"And yours would be...?"

"At your place."

She raised a brow. "The warehouse?"

"Yeah."

Okay...

"The way I figure it, they won't expect us to go back there."

"But if they've tagged the car..."

"Which is why we need to go back into town."

She squinted at him.

"Taxi."

"Ah."

He wanted to ditch the Camaro in town and hail a taxi to take them to the warehouse.

She supposed it could work.

"And after that?"

He held her gaze for a long moment. "After that will come after that."

Right.

Ask a stupid question… She settled back into the seat.

"You ready?"

"Circle around one more time first, please."

"Half a time."

"Deal."

6

JONATHON DIDN'T KID himself into thinking Mara wouldn't make a run for it the first chance she got. But there were a few things he needed to do outside where he could keep an eye on her. So after ditching the Camaro in a shopping center parking lot, calling a taxi to pick them up three blocks away and collecting his Jeep from the warehouse without incident, he headed for a fleabag motel a half hour out of town, on the fringes of Flagstaff, the type that nailed the furniture to the floor and walls to prevent anyone from making off with it. He checked them into a room near the office where he could keep an eye on anyone coming or going.

"Gee, last of the big spenders," Mara said as he opened the door and allowed her to go in first.

"I'm thinking you've seen worse."

She gave him one of those knowing glances that made him unable to blink. "Much."

He closed and locked the door, then checked the

bathroom. No windows except the one next to the door. Good.

He came back out to find her turning on the TV. It was set to automatically air a porn channel. The room filled with the sound of sweaty flesh smacking, groans and moans. He watched her look at the bed behind them. One. A queen size with a ratty-looking dark bedspread.

"Wonder what a blue light would reveal," she said quietly.

He stripped the spread off to reveal white sheets and the scent of bleach.

"I'm going to hit the shower." She walked in the direction of the bathroom, stripping off her shirt as she went.

Good. He was hoping she'd say that. The quicker she did her business, the quicker he could get on with his.

Ten minutes later she was out and dripping in nothing but a towel.

His mouth went instantly dry and he nearly dropped the remote where he'd been checking local stations for any news on what had gone down at the sheriff's office. There was nothing. He'd been hoping to see that the deputy and desk sergeant were okay…and the two gunmen were out of the picture.

"Done," she said.

Her hair was slicked back and looked black when it was wet, bringing out the paleness of her skin and the green in her eyes and emphasizing the rest of her features to a distracting degree.

Yes, he'd known she was attractive. He'd felt that white-hot spark when they'd bumped into each other at the airport. But this…the way she looked now, all dewy and wet, her lips full and plump, her eyes wide and full of sexy suggestion…

He swallowed hard.

"Are you going to get dressed?" he asked.

"Are we sleeping here?"

"Yeah."

"Then no."

Good God Almighty.

Suddenly, what he'd had in mind didn't seem like such a good idea. Not anymore. Not because it didn't appeal to him, but because it appealed too much.

She sat on the bed and opened the small bottle of lotion she'd brought in from the bathroom.

"You need any of this?" she asked.

He shook his head.

"Good. Because that soap dried out my skin something terrible."

Her skin didn't look dry at all. It looked moist and soft and warm and all too touchable.

Oh, boy.

"You want me to apply some to your back?" he asked.

She looked at him skeptically, then smiled. "Sure." She held out the bottle.

He took it, telling himself his hand wasn't trembling because he was about to make contact with her, but because…

Why?

Aw, hell.

He tipped a bit of the lotion out as she shifted to sit on the edge of the bed, moving her damp hair out of the way, revealing the tattoo he'd only caught a glimpse of earlier.

It was a phoenix rising. A Mayan one. And the wings spanned from one shoulder to the other.

"What…? Oh. The tat," she said, talking to him over her shoulder.

Jon's gaze traveled from the sexy curve of her back above the towel still wrapped around her, up over her shoulder to fasten on her profile. Her dark lashes were lowered, her lips lush and oh, so kissable.

"I got it when I was sixteen."

Sixteen.

Her words served as a reminder of both how different they were…and who they were.

At sixteen he'd been arguing with his parents about how often he could drive the car they'd bought him for his birthday. Tattoos had been the furthest thing from his mind.

He hesitated, holding his hands just above her skin. He swore he could feel her heat breach the distance, tempting him in more ways than one. He found his fingers running over her skin a little too easily, making him forget what his intention had been the instant he'd seen her open the tiny bottle.

But now he remembered. So he clamped the cuff on her right wrist, pulled it above her head, thread the other cuff through the bedpost then fastened it to her other wrist.

Her answering laugh surprised him with its full genuineness.

"Oops," she said. "Looks like maybe I should have gotten dressed...."

She hadn't fought him during the cuffing process, but it stood to reason it wouldn't take much to loosen the towel she wore. And the way she now rested across the bed, her hands above her head, her long legs crossed, lent a certain kind of sexy suggestiveness that made his jeans instantly tighten across the crotch. She moved and the towel, indeed, came loose, now dipping just south of a rosy-tipped nipple.

"Care to give a girl a hand?" she asked, pretending an innocence he suspected she didn't possess.

He cocked a brow, then stripped the top sheet from the bed and covered her with it.

She tsked. "Not what I had in mind."

He ignored her as he grabbed the car keys from the top of the TV.

"What's the matter, soldier? Never seen a woman's breast before?"

He eyed her. "You might want to consider getting some shut-eye since I don't know when we'll be on the road again."

Another shift of her leg and the sheet was down...

and so was the towel. "I can think of something else beds are made for…"

So could he.

That was the problem.

He left the room without saying another word, slamming the door shut behind him.

MARA FELT MORE TURNED ON than she had been in a good long while. She figured it was a mix of the earlier adrenaline rush, the protective tendencies of her captor and just plain having gone without for a good long while.

Whatever the reason, her delicates were wetter than they'd gotten during her shower, and the rasp of the sheets against her bare skin when she moved was enough to make her shiver. She squeezed her thighs tightly together, wishing Reece would come back and finish what he'd started.

When he'd touched her back…

She caught her breath at the rush of need that flushed through her veins.

When his fingers had smoothed the lotion over her skin, obviously tracing the outline of her tat, she'd nearly climaxed on the spot.

She tried to reach for the towel, only to be frustrated by the cuffs on her wrists.

Damn.

She repositioned herself and managed to grab the damp towel and toss it to the floor next to the bed.

Yes…that was much better.

She snuggled back down against the sheet, rubbing her bare legs together so the friction added to the dampness. She wished she could touch herself, but then again, there was something delicious about not being able to. She rolled to the left, then the right, brushing against the top sheet that had bunched down around her waist. She wriggled until she could reach the sheet with her teeth, pulling it up between her breasts and working it so it was between her legs.

Mmm...yeah.

She didn't know where Reece had gone or when he'd be back, but she planned to make good use of the time. She rocked her hips back and forth, pressing her pelvis against the mattress as best she could given her awkward position. Heat swelled over her in waves....

She told herself she should be thinking her way out of her current circumstances. But, damn it, she'd been thinking about nothing but that for what seemed like so long, she wanted...no, *needed,* to think about something else for a little while.

Besides, she knew there was nothing like a good, solid orgasm to help relieve stress and oil her brain cells.

She allowed images to float through her mind.

Bumping into Reece at the airport...

Kissing him when she'd cuffed him back at the warehouse...

The feel of his fingertips against the sensitive skin of her back...

The way he'd looked at her breast as if he'd like nothing more than to lick it…

Imagining his tongue against more than her nipple…

She squeezed her thighs tightly together and gasped.

There. Yes, right there!

Yes!

7

JONATHON SAT IN THE DINER across the parking lot from the restaurant drinking a cup of coffee, his eyes trained on the door to motel room #3, the cell phone sitting on the table in front of him. The insistent drum of his pulse had nothing to do with the fear of Mara leaving, and everything to do with the fear of her staying.

Never, ever, in the two years he and Julie had been a couple, had he felt such overwhelming need for another woman.

Then again, Mara wasn't just another woman. She was a fugitive. A suspect for murder.

He took a deep breath, wondering why the information was doing absolutely nothing to cool his libido.

But he knew one thing that would.

He finally pulled his cell phone closer.

Fifty-four missed calls, thirty-three voice-mail messages and over a hundred texts.

All from Julie.

Well, at least he was pretty sure they were all from Julie.

He picked up the cell again and quickly scrolled through the logs. Wait, there was a call from Lazarus. He checked voice messages. No message.

Damn.

The call had come in around the time he'd been at the sheriff's office.

He absently rubbed his forehead.

"Fill up?" the waitress asked.

He nudged his cup toward her.

"Sure I can't interest you in something to eat?"

"Maybe later."

"Just wave for me when you're ready."

He indicated he would and she left him alone again.

There weren't very many patrons in the diner at that hour. Maybe five others, most at the counter watching a TV perched in the corner near the ceiling. He glanced at it from time to time to see if there was any local coverage of what had gone down at the Winslow sheriff's office. But it was tuned in to a national sports channel and broadcasting a baseball double header featuring teams he'd normally be following. But tonight, he barely registered the score.

He sipped his coffee and accessed the first voice mail.

The sound of Julie's voice set his teeth on edge, even though she sounded calm enough.

"Hello? It's me. Just thought I'd tell you I'm fine,

you know, in case you cared. Got the dry cleaning off okay. Back home. Call me the instant you get this."

By the time he got to voice mail ten, he'd had enough. She'd progressively gotten angrier and more accusatory.

"I don't know where you are, or who you're with, but I just thought I'd let you know your dog pooped on my side of the bed then dragged his butt against my pillow. Your mom called wanting to know if we were coming for that stupid thirtieth anniversary party she's having next month and I told her I had that five-year high school reunion thing so we probably wouldn't. She got snippy with me. Imagine the nerve! I mean, your father died years ago. She's not really married to him anymore. I knew she never liked me. Oh, and to top it off, I broke a nail, my regular girl wasn't in and the woman who took her appointments completely screwed it up! I certainly hope you're having a good day, because I'm not..."

He'd stopped the message there and pressed the button to empty the remaining ones from the queue. If that's how she was at message ten, he could only imagine what number thirty-three sounded like.

He did the same with the texts without reading them, then put the cell phone down, staring at it,

When had things gotten so volatile between them?

He winced. Had Julie really told his mother they wouldn't go to her party? Spoken for him without consulting with him first? Bettina Reece must have been shocked.

While he and his mother certainly had their issues, his mom was the salt of the earth, the epitome of propriety. That's why her words about Julie at a Fourth of July family BBQ rang clearly in his head: "Jonny, you know I'm the last one to say anything bad about a body, but..."

She'd trailed off.

"But?" he'd asked, giving her a hand cleaning up in the kitchen. Julie had been back in his old bedroom catching a nap because the day had been so "tiresome" for her.

"But...it might be a good idea to leave Julie home next time you come for a visit. She doesn't seem to like it here much."

He'd brushed off the suggestion, made excuses for Julie—she was in a transition from working every day at school to summer break, something or other having to do with her own mother, whom she seemed to bicker with constantly—and quickly changed the subject.

It hadn't struck him then what his mother had been saying. She wasn't suggesting he not bring her home because Julie might be happier staying behind. No, she was politely suggesting she not come because the family didn't want her there.

Wow!

He lifted his cup only to find he'd already downed the contents.

He waved for the waitress to give him a refill and forced himself to clear his mind. He'd come to the diner to get a better handle on his professional life, not to review his personal one.

Still…

He scrolled to Julie's number, pressed the button that would allow him to leave a voice-mail message for her, and simply said he was fine, that he hoped she was, too, and that he'd talk to her soon, hopefully tomorrow. Good night.

It was only after he'd disconnected that he realized he hadn't said "I love you."

That was telling….

He shook his head and accessed the internet on his cell phone, logging on to the secure server for Lazarus and entering Mara's name for a background check.

His cell alerted him to an incoming call.

Julie.

He pressed the button to refuse it and continued.

Another call.

He refused it again. But this time, he suspended his online search and went to the menu that would allow him to refuse all of Julie's calls, so she'd be put straight through to voice mail. Then he set the system up so he wouldn't be alerted to any new messages.

Finally he could continue his search.

Two additional cups of coffee later, his stomach growled at him over the sound of his own buzzing thoughts.

Mara Lynn Findlay, aka Ruby Gloom, aka Iona Skye and a host of other less memorable names, wasn't a real person. She couldn't be. Instead, her past read like something out of a fiction novel. Aside from two felonies she'd been convicted of as a teen, both of which had been expunged from her official record but still available to Lazarus sources, her criminal past read like a road map to a lifetime in prison.

Or at least, to the crime of which she was currently accused.

At sixteen, she'd not only gotten that tattoo, but she'd also been arrested with a handful of other rebels who were part of a well-known, southwest militia. He came across photos of her then, wearing fatigues much like those worn by the two gunmen at the sheriff's earlier, and was armed with guns in much the same way. In one of the shots, she was arm in arm with a guy dressed the same, beaming up at him like the sun itself rose and set on him.

He squinted, wishing his cell screen were larger.

Out of simple curiosity, he did a background check on one certain Gerald Butler.

The man known as "The General" to his comrades.

Right. He grimaced. How in the hell had Mara gotten mixed up with people like that?

Ah, yes. It appeared "The General" currently resided in a federal pen awaiting trial for crimes against the government and, shocker, murder.

He filed the information away and went on to the next bit.

If the previous data saddened him, this one surprised him. Mara had served a stint in the army....

His cell rang.

He didn't recognize the number.

"Hello?"

"Oh, my God! He answered…"

Julie.

What in the hell?

He grit his back teeth together, motioned for the waitress then pressed Mute while he placed an order.

"Oh, wait a minute." Did Mara like pie? "A piece of that blackberry, too. To go."

"You got it, sugar."

Silence on the phone. "Where *are* you? And who just called you sugar?" Julie demanded.

Jon didn't bother explaining. He didn't have to. He knew she'd be off on her next rant within the span of breath it would take him to try to explain, anyway.

And, indeed, she was.

He decided she had whatever time it took for his burger to get there then he was cutting her off. Until then, he half listened to her, half stared at the door to motel room #3, wondering what Mara Lynn Findlay was doing right that very minute…and whether or not he'd walk in and find her naked….

8

J ON RETURNED TO THE motel room to find Mara fast asleep, without a towel, and totally, gloriously uncovered....

He stood in the open doorway incapable of movement, caught between wanting to slam the door shut and staying quiet so as not to disturb her.

Damn, but she was sexy as hell....

She lay with her hips turned toward him, her left leg over her right to keep him from seeing too much. But her arms were still above her head attached to the board with the cuffs, leaving her breasts bare and open to his hungry gaze.

Never, ever, had he returned to the house he shared with Julie and found her sleeping like that. First of all, if she was waiting for him, she wouldn't have been asleep. Second of all, she'd have catapulted from the bed the instant she heard him, anxious to fill him in on every minute detail of her day, whether he cared or not.

Mara...

Well, Mara had been handcuffed to the bed by him and still managed to not only fall asleep, but look damn good doing it.

His gaze skimmed over her, from her tousled hair and curvy hip to her shapely calves and purple-painted toenails. Hunger hit him so strong, a hundred double-size cheeseburgers wouldn't have been unable to satisfy him.

He considered the bag of food in his hand, then put it down next to the TV before quietly closing the door. There was only one bed in the room. He could sleep in the uncomfortable-looking chair, but Mara was restrained and the bed was big. He figured he should be able to get in a good night's sleep without worrying too much. When it came to self-control, all he'd have to do was remember Julie. Thoughts of her would be like a bucket full of ice poured down the front of his boxers.

He pulled off his T-shirt and laid it over the chair. Then he took off his boots and socks before going into the bathroom to clean up and brush his teeth using a bag of supplies he'd picked up from a drugstore across the street. He put on deodorant, ran his damp hands through his hair then went into the other room and shut off the TV and the light before carefully lying on the very edge of the bed next to Mara.

He found his gaze drawn to her beautifully bare form again. Then he silently cursed himself, before throwing the top sheet over her, nearly covering her head, as well. She made a soft sound and shifted, but didn't wake.

He was immensely grateful.

If a sleeping Mara did this to him, he could only imagine what an awake one could do.

No, he didn't have to imagine; he knew. She'd nearly shredded his intentions to handcuff her earlier with just a couple of soft hums of approval as he smoothed lotion on her back.

Jon positioned pillows behind him so he was half sitting up, then joined his forearms behind his head, staring at the ceiling. Was it him, or did she smell good? Quite a feat, considering she'd used the cheap motel soaps and shampoo. Yet there you had it.

He closed his eyes and swallowed hard, mentally reviewing what he'd learned about her and her situation. When his thoughts started straying again, he threw a shot of Julie into the mix. Was it too much to hope that she wouldn't find another friend's phone to call him? At this point, he wanted to keep the ringer on in case Lazarus called again.

He stretched his neck and counted backward from a hundred. Only, when he got to ten, he upgraded the number to a thousand....

The instant daylight broke, he intended to make arrangements to turn Mara over to federal officials as soon as humanly possible. The quicker the naked little temptress was out of his life, the better all the way around....

PURE, ANIMAL NEED FILLED HIM from the groin outward....

Jon stretched and thrust his hips against an unknown source of pleasure, his erection thick and puls-
ing.

He groaned, not wanting to wake from the dream,
but knowing he had to. If only because he was afraid
of who he'd find himself having sex with in his sleep.

The trouble was, the sensations didn't dissipate
when he groggily opened his eyes. Indeed, they intensified.

If only because it wasn't a dream.

Somehow Mara had freed herself from the cuffs,
opened his jeans and was slowly stroking his long,
hard length with her fingers.

Damn, how...?

She seemed to register he was no longer asleep.
But rather than stop, she continued stroking him. He
was trapped between wanting, needing to break away
from her and wanting, needing for her to continue....

Julie, Julie, Julie...

He was a breath away from rolling off the bed when
Mara slid her mouth over the head of his cock.

Sweet heaven...

How long had it been since he'd had a woman's
mouth on him? Long before meeting Julie, who
thought oral sex unsanitary. She wouldn't even allow
him south of her border.

Mara slid her lips down the inside length of his

erection, then licked her way back up before taking him into her mouth and sucking lightly.

Any thoughts of his girlfriend fled from his head as quickly as common sense and his body happily took over. Oh, yes, how he'd missed this. And if the fact that it was Mara providing the pleasure factored in to his heightened reaction, he wasn't nearly ready to admit it. All he knew was he wanted her to continue. *Please.*

She withdrew her attention.

He groaned in protest, then felt her patting around in his jeans pockets.

"What…what are you looking for?"

"You can't tell me you don't have… Bingo!"

MARA FELT LIKE a kid on Christmas morning.

She opened the foil packet with her teeth, rolled the lubricated latex down over Reece's hot, hard shaft then straddled him. She couldn't remember a time when she'd wanted anything so very much. She wanted to feel him inside her so desperately, she couldn't think straight.

"Wait," he rasped, grasping her hips. "I don't think this is a good idea…."

She licked her parched lips, then leaned down to kiss him. When he kissed back with as much fervor as she demonstrated, she knew he wanted this as much as she did.

"Oh?" she whispered. "Because I think this is the best idea I've had in a long, long—" she reached between her thighs and positioned him against her, sliding down over him in one, bone-shivering stroke "—time."

Oh, this felt so very good.

He felt so very good.

Her earlier orgasm had been uniquely powerful in that she'd never experienced one to that degree without use of her hands. And usually a man was required. But she'd been so thoroughly sated, she'd drifted off into a sound sleep and hadn't even heard Reece return to the room. But when she'd woken up a little while ago to the sound of his soft snores next to her...well, that physical need had erupted in her all over again, even stronger now that she felt him beside her.

She'd used her earring to pick the cuffs by straightening the dangling hook wire, and hadn't been able to keep herself from touching him. He was such a perfect male specimen. Every part of him was buff and shined. But it was when she'd brushed the tips of her fingertips against the slight bulge in the front of his jeans, and felt his immediate, unconscious, primal response that she knew there was no turning back.

She knew he wanted her. She'd viewed the physical need in his blue eyes the moment they'd met at the airport. She'd felt it in his hands when he'd smoothed the lotion over her back.

Oh, she suspected he had a girlfriend. And she guessed that part of what he'd needed to do when he'd left the room earlier was maybe to patch things up with her. But just then, she didn't care. All that mattered was this moment. Feeling him fill her to overflowing.

She leaned down to kiss him again, surprised and warmed when he cupped her face to bring her closer. His kiss was deep and soulful and hungry. And made her even hotter.

She reluctantly broke free, then braced her hands against his shoulders, rocking her hips forward.

Wow!

She did it again…and again…feeling him touch her everywhere, yet nowhere…. Her breathing grew ragged and her heart thrummed a rhythm so loud she could hear nothing beyond it.

She leaned forward to kiss him again, lingeringly. Then he gently pressed his hand against her shoulder, easing her back up, presumably so he could watch her.

And she'd thought she was turned on before…. She leaned back even farther, bracing her hands against his rock-hard thighs, and rode him slow and easy. His fingers moved over her sex, up her trembling stomach, then gently touched her breasts. She caught his hand and held it there, shivering as he lightly pinched her nipple.

"God, you feel so good," he said, murmuring the exact same words she'd thought just moments before.

She couldn't say how long they'd stayed like that— her on top…him stroking and caressing her—but her movements began to quicken, as if her body was eager to reach the release she'd promised. Reece followed suit, grasping her hips tightly and thrusting upward, long, hard strokes that left her breathless….

"I'm close," she moaned softly. "So close… Come with me."

His fingers grasped her tighter. "Already there."

9

"So what did you mean when you asked me that question?" Jon inquired.

A long time after he'd first awakened to the wet dream of Mara touching him, he lay back, one arm behind his head because Lord only knew where all the pillows had gone, the blankets, too, for that matter. Mara was curved against his side, her bare, damp pelvis resting solidly against his hip.

It had taken some work to move his mind beyond sounds to actually form full words. These past few hours had been...

Words escaped him again merely thinking about it.

Mara was so, open, mind-blowingly sexual...

"Which one?" Her response brought his halting thoughts to a stop.

"The first one you asked me."

He lazily stroked her back from the tat to her bottom, then back again. She was smooth and sexy and hotter than any woman he'd ever known.

Julie briefly entered his mind but he quickly ousted her. Because the answer also applied to her, no matter how unfair that sounded. And this time with Mara, well, it existed as time outside of time. It wasn't reality. While he didn't excuse himself for what they'd just done, and understood there would be consequences, so long as he was in the moment, he surrendered to staying there.

Staying with Mara.

"I'm still not following you," she said quietly, running her tongue slowly over his nipple.

His muscles contracted. Who knew the male nipple could be as sensitive as a female's? He sure as hell hadn't.

He cleared his throat, hoping it would help clear his mind. "When you inquired as to why I hadn't asked whether you committed the crime."

Her movements ceased.

Uh-oh.

He sensed he'd said something wrong.

When she began to roll away, he knew he had.

He held her firm with his hand against her back.

"I've got to use the restroom," she said quietly.

She'd just gone a little while ago, so he wasn't buying it. "Nice try. Answer me. Please."

She fell silent, then took a long breath, lolling her head to rest against his arm. "Do you really want to ruin this afterglow?"

He grinned. "I'm thinking it will take a lot more than a simple question to do that."

She looked at him in the dark. "That's because there's nothing simple about it. Or the answer."

He shifted slightly so her head lay at a better angle. "Now it's me who's not following you."

"The question. The answer."

He remained quiet, giving her the room she needed to explain. He figured it was a good sign that she was no longer trying to roll away.

Finally, she said, "Gut instincts. Rules. Roles. What's important."

"Go on," he said.

"People should always come first."

He put what little she'd said with what he already knew about her. "Ah. So you're arguing Anarchy v. Law."

"No," she said slowly. "Truth v. Lies."

She moved again. This time he let her. He joined his other hand behind his head and stared at the ceiling, aware of her folding her arms behind her head and sharing his ceiling contemplation.

"The first question I would have asked, you know, had our roles been reversed, is had you done it," she said.

"And how would you have known if I was telling the truth?"

"I wouldn't."

He squinted at her. That made no sense at all.

"But I would have a good idea of whether you had or not. And, simple courtesy dictates that you at least give a body the benefit of the doubt before trying and convicting them."

"Ah, but that's the law."

She smiled at him. "Yes, it is. And it would be a better world if everyone followed that particular one."

"Except in this matter, you're asking me to play judge and jury."

"How so?"

"By finding you innocent."

She fell silent.

"You see, it's not my job to decide your guilt or innocence either way. It's my job to bring you to stand before those who will."

"For money."

He nodded. "For money."

"So how does that make you any different than the criminal?"

"Oh, I don't know. No one gets shot?"

She lightly swatted him.

He didn't say anything for a long time. He merely stayed there, listening to her breathing.

She eventually said, "That's the thinking that got me into trouble with the military."

He took in her profile, remembering the reference he'd seen about her having served.

"Dishonorably discharged," she said, answering his question before he could ask.

"For…"

"Going AWOL. And convincing five of my fellow soldiers to come with me."

He raised his brows and then chuckled. "Hot party somewhere?"

"In Iraq?" She shook her head. "Not likely. I disagreed with my orders."

"Which were?"

"To play executioner without the target being offered a fair trial. He was a man in the neighborhood we were responsible for."

"You were ordered to kill him?"

"Yes."

"So instead, you set him free."

"No. I refused to kill him."

He didn't respond.

She rolled to face him. "He was a father of six, all under the age of ten. It was a time of war. I don't care what he did, short of mass murder—which wasn't the case. If any of us had committed a like crime, we would have come home to ribbons and parades."

"Did you?" he asked.

"Did I what?"

"Come home to ribbons and parades."

She stared at him. "Did you?"

He had. His mother had made sure of that. She'd brought out the Army Reserve Band and the media and the entire family when he'd come home.

"Yeah, thought so."

"You have a problem with my mom welcoming her youngest son home?"

"I have a problem with the double standard." She lay back down. "My father once told me, 'The only thing worth anything is your word. So if you say it, you'd damn well better do it. Walk your talk, and talk your walk.'"

He couldn't recall seeing anything about her father in the data he'd scanned. Where had the man been when Mara was sixteen, getting that tat and signing up with the local militia?

Or maybe her dad was the one who got her involved....

"And how is that not walking my talk?"

"I'm referring to my court martial and ultimate discharge," she said. "Here we salute our flag and all she supposedly stands for—freedom, justice and the American way."

"I think that's Superman," he interrupted.

She stared at him. "You know what I mean."

Sadly, he did.

He'd noticed the double standard throughout his own tour overseas. Nearly every fundamental tenet of the American Constitution was broken at some point or another.

But it was war. And the only order that counted was the order that came from above. If not for them...well, there would be nothing but chaos.

"A man is only as good as the man leading him," he said.

"No, a man is only as good as he is. Period."

He winced.

If he looked at it that way, he'd have an awful lot to apologize for.

Thankfully he didn't share her viewpoint. While he appreciated it, maybe even admired it in some sort of rebellious way, he sided with the law. Humans didn't survive this long by continuing to beat each other over the heads with spiked clubs.

He shifted to look at her in the dim light. Who was this woman? He recalled the photo of the girl looking up in idol worship at the militia guy at her side.

"Are your parents alive?" he asked quietly.

Her brows came together briefly. "My mom is. She's living over in Santa Fe somewhere. She's an artist."

"And your dad?"

He noticed the way her chin dug into chest, a protective maneuver meant to cover but instead revealed. "He went MIA in Bosnia. Assumed dead."

"Which branch?"

"Army. Of course."

He smiled. Of course.

That explained how her anarchist little heart had ended up in the military in the first place.

Still, it didn't explain how she'd ended up with a scumbag like Butler.

"How about yours?" she asked.

"Mine?"

"Your parents. Still with us?"

"Mom, yes. Dad unfortunately passed a few years ago."

"I'm sorry."

"Thanks."

She didn't ask and he didn't volunteer how he'd died. Truth was, he still wasn't good at sharing the story of how he'd lost his father. It had been a shock, right out of left field. He'd had a massive coronary. The autopsy had read that he'd had major blockages in three of his major arteries, something his regular check-ups hadn't found because he'd been in such excellent shape otherwise. He'd been a marathon runner, a swimmer, a golfer. You name it, if it was something to do outside, his dad did it.

Yet it hadn't helped him escape death when it came knocking.

His cell phone rang on the end table. He glanced at the clock. It was just after 2:00 a.m.

Couldn't be good news.

He picked it up and read the display—the same "friend" number Julie had used earlier.

Damn.

He added the number to the Refuse list and put the cell phone back down.

Silence reigned for a while. Then he heard Mara's soft laugh.

"I take it that was Julie?"

Jon closed his eyes and rubbed his lids. He didn't have to ask how she knew. When she'd held him captive at the warehouse earlier, she'd surely gotten a look at his cell display.

"Yeah," he admitted.

"So, are you going to marry her?"

10

REECE WENT INTO A COUGHING fit so violent Mara ran to the bathroom to get him water. She stopped short of smacking him on the back, but just barely. She turned on the light, as much for him to see the cup as for her to see the expression on his face.

Yep, he was shocked.

She fought the urge to smile.

"I take it that means no," she said quietly.

Reece gulped the water and then dragged his wrist across his mouth. "You take it correctly."

Mara picked up the towel and wrapped it around herself, although she was completely comfortable sitting there nude. "But she is your girlfriend."

His grimace told her that his problems with Julie-with-a-Heart predated her entering his life.

Good. She didn't like the thought of being the other woman.

Although technically she wasn't. They were merely

two ships passing in the night. He was a military gunner; she was a pirate ship.

And she fully intended to outrun, outwit and outplay him.

Of course, that didn't mean she couldn't enjoy him while she was at it. And, oh, boy, was she enjoying him.

He sat up on the other side of the bed, then got up and stood into his jeans before going into the bathroom and closing the door.

Mara sat back against the headboard and waited for him. This was far too interesting to let slip.

A good fifteen minutes passed before he finally came out shaking water from his hands, his hair damp. She knew he hadn't taken a shower. She would have heard him if he had. Rather, she could imagine him standing there, staring into the mirror for a good long while before splashing cold water on his face.

"Would you rather not talk about it?" she asked, incapable of stopping the smile that threatened.

"I'd rather not, thanks."

She patted the spot next to her. "Tough. Come tell me."

He glowered at her. "Not a chance."

"Not a chance you'll get back into bed with me? Or that you'll tell me about Julie?"

"Both."

He put his T-shirt on.

"I'm going for coffee. You want some?"

She shook her head. "Nope."

He fastened his shoulder holster and grabbed his keys and cell phone. "I'll be back."

"When?"

"When I'm back."

She laughed.

He slammed the door after himself.

WHAT IN THE HELL was he doing?

Jon asked himself the question over and again as he walked aimlessly....

Just yesterday he'd been a guy hoping for a solo assignment that would change his professional life. He'd intended to live happily ever after with what he'd believed was the girl of his dreams. Instead, he'd gotten a job that had turned his personal life upside down and made him realize Julie was a nightmare.

But what did that make Mara?

A wet dream?

He ran his hand over his hair as he glanced at his watch. He was aware he'd left Mara back at the motel unrestrained and alone. But at this point, he didn't think she was going anywhere. He didn't know how he knew, but he did.

Still, he didn't think it a good idea to leave her by herself for too long in case she decided to consider her options.

He bought two coffees to go from the all-night diner and walked across the lot to room #3. Opening the door, he encountered much the same scene as he had a few hours before: Mara was fast asleep on her side of the bed. The difference was she was covered by a sheet…and her hands were free.

He put the coffee down next to the bag of food he'd gotten earlier, slightly amused to find she'd taken a couple of bites out of the burger and finished the pie.

He walked to her side of the bed, glancing down at her sleeping face.

Damn.

It probably would have been better not to look.

Mara wasn't beautiful by any stretch. Her features were too unusual. Her eyes were too large, her nose too small, her mouth almost too generous. But she was animated even at rest. And there was an electricity about her that mesmerized him. Her information sheet said she was a natural blonde, but you couldn't tell by looking at her red hair now. He tried to image her otherwise and couldn't. She seemed more of a redhead or a brunette than a blonde.

Then again, who was he to say? He'd thought Julie was an angel when he first met her.

And he'd even considered marrying her.

So why hadn't he proposed?

He was looking at the reason why.

Oh, not because he was under any misconception that he was in love with Mara. But he had slept with her. For that reason alone, he knew he couldn't marry Julie.

The woman he married would keep him from wanting to sleep with anyone else.

But why hadn't he taken the leap before he met Mara?

He realized that perhaps, deep down, he'd always known his and Julie's paths would part.

He quietly walked to the other side of the bed and sat down heavily in the only chair in the room, propping his elbows on his knees.

What was he doing?

Sure, in his late teens, early twenties, he'd certainly known his share of women. He'd dated frequently and hadn't thought much about taking sex where it was offered. But that was back then.

And, well...he'd lived with Julie.

He couldn't help noticing he'd used the past tense, and his brain froze.

Yes, okay, it was over. It probably had been for a while. It was just taking a while for him to catch up with the truth. Things hadn't been good between them for a long time. In fact, things probably hadn't been good even before they'd rented the small house together on the outskirts of Colorado Springs two months ago. But he'd loved her and so he'd gone ahead.

He caught his unconscious word choice again.

Did he really not love her anymore?

No. He loved her. He was just no longer in love with her.

He groaned inwardly and rubbed his hands over his face. What in the hell was happening to him? He sounded like a woman, for God's sake.

Whatever was going on, he decided he didn't much like this emotional stuff.

So what did he do? Did he go back to Colorado

Springs and tell Julie he was moving out? Their lease was month-to-month, so he could probably pack a bag and bunk with one of the guys at Lazarus until he found his own place. Of course, he'd kick in for the final month's rent.

Was it enough time? Would she be upset?

He realized the snort he heard was his own. Of course she was going to be upset. *Upset* was her middle name. This, however, might be worthy of a nuclear meltdown. And it might very well involve lawyers.

He stared straight ahead. Would she do that? Yes, he fully expected she would.

Not that it would stop him from breaking things off.

He scratched the back of his head, wondering if it was really just last week that he'd been considering a Christmas Day proposal a few months from now.

His gaze settled on the sleeping form of the woman who had changed his life.

Or, rather, opened his eyes to the truth.

Mara dozed away as if she hadn't a care in the world, when, in fact, her cares were heavier than most. And definitely more complicated than his.

Damn, but she was sexier than hell. Merely remembering the way she'd ridden him, her back arched, breasts high, her breath coming in humming gasps…

He was rock-hard all over again.

He sat back and folded his hands over his stomach. Funny, despite all the talking they'd done earlier about her "question," she had never answered the question herself. Then again, she really hadn't had to. He knew her answer would be "no, she didn't do it."

And, strangely enough, he believed her.

Of course, what that meant in the larger scheme of things, he didn't know.

Yes, he did. It meant he wouldn't be surrendering her to the nearest federal courthouse at first light.

He waited for reason to weigh in.

Nothing.

Instead, he felt a total sense of calm, certainty that he was doing the right thing.

No, he wasn't letting her go. To do so would be nothing short of insane. Not merely because of his job, but because she was obviously in major trouble. Knowing what he did now, he had little doubt those two men at the sheriff's office were members of the same militia to which she'd once belonged.

He also had no doubt that they'd been there to kill her.

To leave her now, well, while he didn't view her as anything close to helpless, everyone could use a little help now and again.

At any rate, his brain was beginning to register the strains of extra innings.

The question now was whether he dared crawl back into that bed with her.

He heard her soft snore and smiled.

Yes, yes, he did.

11

MARA'S FACE WAS WARM. She blinked open her eyes to the sunlight, then clamped them shut. Too bright.

She smiled and rolled over, feeling better than she had in a good, long while. Like a cat that had been properly fed, had its belly rubbed and was now stretched out in sated bliss.

Then her circumstances washed over her and she jackknifed upright.

"Good morning."

She looked to find Reece sitting in the chair drinking coffee and reading what looked like a newspaper.

She squinted, trying to slow her heart rate. On a sliding scale, she was mightily glad she'd woken up to him rather than the alternative. Still, there was something wrong with this picture. It was… It was…

A little too normal. Too…domestic.

"I got one for you if you want it," he said, gesturing to a second coffee cup.

Dangerous. Very definitely dangerous. It wasn't just

the fact that she'd slept so soundly, without thought to what was going on around her that worried her. No, something within her was reacting to Reece in a way with which she was unfamiliar.

It was a toss-up as to which was more dangerous.

Mara stripped off the sheet, leaving herself obviously bare. She enjoyed his automatic stare as she got up and slowly walked to the table to take the second cup. If she was trying to reset the tone back to sex and awe…well, that was between her and her still-tingling thighs.

"Thanks," she said.

She was fully aware the curtains were open and anyone walking by could see her if they looked. It made Reece's attention all the hotter.

She took a long sip from the extralarge takeout cup. "Just as I like it. Strong and black." She reached for the paper. "Anything interesting?"

He moved it out of her reach then showed her the cover article. Melee at Winslow Sheriff's Office: Deputy Injured. Two Unknown Suspects, Considered Armed And Dangerous, On the Loose.

There was a grainy photo of the two suspects.

Mara took another sip of coffee. "You'd think they'd have better security cameras."

"You can say that again."

"At least no one's dead."

"The sheriff's deputy is in critical condition."

Mara's hand stilled.

"No mention of our presence," he said.

She began walking toward the bathroom. "What does that matter? I'm wanted for a capital crime already."

"Yes, you are."

She looked over her shoulder to find him reading the paper rather than looking at her ass as she'd hoped. She gathered her clothes, then went into the bathroom and turned on the shower. But instead of climbing right in, she stood for a moment leaning against the wall, staring into the building steam.

She hated the thought that someone had been hurt because of her. While she could argue until she was blue in the face that she'd warned Reece not to go there, the fact was that deputy was in pain because those gunmen had been after her.

She hoped he recovered.

A part of her whispered she should be glad she wasn't on the receiving end of those bullets.

She climbed into the shower. But she wasn't in there a minute before Reece was ripping the shower curtain open—for reasons that had nothing to do with sex.

"FBI HAS CAUGHT UP WITH US."

Jon grabbed a towel and thrust it at her, trying not to notice how the water sluiced over the tips of Mara's breasts down to between her thighs.

Aw, hell.

One moment he'd been reading the newspaper—or trying to, considering thoughts of a naked Mara mere feet away taking a shower had proved one hell of a distraction—and the next, he had watched a dark SUV drive into the parking lot in front of the motel office. Two dark-suited men with dark sunglasses had gotten out, incapable of looking more like federal agents had they flashed their IDs in his direction.

Mara took the towel and was out of the shower quicker than he'd have thought possible. "What's the plan?"

Jon had closed the curtains over the front window, but his Jeep was parked directly in front. And he had little doubt that he was the reason the FBI had found them there. Likely there had been footage of him and Mara at the Winslow sheriff's office after all, only it hadn't been for public consumption. The way facial identification programs were today, he suspected it would take very little to put his face together with his name. And once they did that...

Well, he'd paid for the room with his Lazarus credit card.

As he had the Jeep.

Damn.

Mara rushed into the room and was dressed faster than a firefighter on her way to a four-alarm blaze.

"There's only the one exit," he said.

She'd moved toward the window and peeked through the curtains without touching them. "Yes, well, we'd better find another one quick. They're in the office and the clerk is pointing in this direction."

Great.

Jon considered his options. There weren't many.

Then he spotted the air vent in the bathroom ceiling.

He reached for his duffel and took out the toolkit, finding the necessary screwdriver. He went to work on the vent screws.

"That's barely wide enough for me to get through."

"Exactly."

"But…"

There.

He eased out the grate and turned toward her. "Ready?"

"What are you going to do?"

"Whatever it takes."

He told her what he had in mind. She nodded and when he offered her a boost, she took it. Into the vent she went.

A minute later, a knock sounded at the door.

Jon reattached the grate, grabbed the extra coffee cup, the handcuffs and the bottle of lotion and went into the bathroom, where he splashed cold water over his face and hair and was at the door when another knock sounded.

"Jonathon Reece?" the agent on the right said.

"Yes."

He flashed his ID. "FBI. May we come in?"

He opened the door farther and stepped aside.

They walked in, giving the room a once-over.

"Where's Miss Findlay?"

"Your guess is as good as mine," he said. "She got away from me right after the Winslow sheriff's office fiasco last night."

The agents looked at each other, then back at him.

"I don't think I have to tell you her background," Jon added. "Trust me, I'm as unhappy about it as you are. And between us? I'd prefer no one find out. I mean, besides the three of us."

He grimaced and went to get his cup of coffee.

One of the men stepped toward the bathroom door and took a look around, obviously noting the shower had just been used. Jon ran his hand over his wet hair. The agent turned around, directly under the vent. The way his luck was running, Jon half expected one of the screws to come loose and bean the guy on the head. Or a bit of dust to waft down, making him sneeze and look up.

The other one held out a card. "If you catch up with her before we do, call us immediately."

Jon took it. Just a number. No name or identifying agency, although he knew he was dealing with the FBI. "How does that affect my bounty?"

"You'll get it."

"Deal, then."

"Have any idea where she's gone?" the agent on the right asked.

"Well, if I did, I wouldn't tell you, would I? Because your finding her first definitely means no bounty."

They shared another cryptic look and then headed for the door, one following the other out.

Jon stood in the doorway, watching as they climbed into their SUV and sped off.

Shit.

If the FBI was on his tail, he had his work cut out for him.

He finally closed the door and went to stand in front of the vent.

"You still there?"

No answer.

Good.

He looked at his watch, then grabbed his cell phone and the rest of his gear. He had to wait before leaving, just in case the agents he'd spoken with hovered around waiting for him.

Why did he have the feeling those minutes would rank up there with some of the longest of his life?

12

A HALF HOUR LATER, Jon waited at a corner store a mile up the road from the motel. He'd ditched his Jeep a half mile in the other direction and then hiked back.

Only, Mara was nowhere in sight.

He dropped his duffel at his feet and reached for his cell phone. Twenty messages; none from her.

Damn.

He'd been clear on the plan if she found a way out. They'd meet up here in a half hour but wouldn't stick around longer than two hours. That meant he might have a long wait ahead of him. And he accepted it might very well be for naught. There were no guarantees she would show.

He squinted up and down the busy street.

It was just past 8:00 a.m. but he bet the temperature was already over ninety. At one time, he wouldn't have noticed. The heat would have been as normal as the sunrise. Not anymore. He'd adapted to Colorado's climate, making him a lizard without scales here now.

Had Mara ditched him?

Quite possibly.

Not that he could blame her if she had. He'd been the one to lead the FBI to them. He was sure of that.

She had enough to worry about without him making matters worse.

What was he talking about? He was there to take her in, as well.

How in the hell had things gotten so complicated so fast?

A car honked its horn at the curb some yards away. He glanced at it, then away, looking for her. More horn honking. He stared at the dusty old Blazer.

Mara?

He crossed the parking lot and rounded the driver's side. She rolled down the window, smiling at him.

"Get in."

Get in?

He did, fastening himself into the passenger's side moments later.

She backed up and turned into traffic, heading west.

"Where'd you get this?"

She smiled that enigmatic, challenging smile. "I have my sources."

"You didn't steal it?"

"I didn't steal it. Did you see grand theft auto on my rap sheet?"

No, he hadn't. But that didn't mean she wasn't

capable of it. He was sure if the need arose, she'd have a car running without use of the keys in no time.

But he trusted what she said for reasons he wasn't entirely sure of.

"I figure they must have identified you from the sheriff's office," she said. "Traced you to the motel and probably made your rented Jeep."

He nodded. "Yeah. My thoughts exactly."

What it didn't explain was why she'd come back for him.

"So I figured it wouldn't hurt to get fresh wheels."

"Yours?"

"In a manner of speaking."

He stared at her.

"It's titled to one of my mother's friends. One of a few I keep parked around town."

"In case you're wanted for a capital crime?"

The smile left her face.

Jon wanted to take his words back.

He figured her need for backup cars had to do with her off-the-grid militia background. Hell, for all he knew, she didn't even have a valid license. Or if she did, it didn't register the right address or even her real name.

He, on the other hand, rated so many blips on the grid, his just sitting next to her probably put them both in danger.

If the FBI knew who he was and what he was doing, then so did the two guys at the sheriff's office....

He took his cell phone out and popped the battery.

"Figured you would have done that back at the motel," she said, looking at him.

"I should have."

As it was, he could probably be traced to the store, and the surveillance cameras had likely registered her change in wheels.

"Don't worry. I parked outside the range of big brother, and the plates are caked in mud, just like the rest of it."

"Still, I'm sure it won't take them long to figure it out," he said.

He watched her squeeze and release the cracked leather steering wheel. "I'm sure you're right. Which means we need to get on with this."

"With what?"

She looked at him. "Making sure the right person pays for the crime...."

MARA HEADED OUT OF TOWN then pointed the Blazer north. She didn't kid herself into thinking her plan was going to be easy. If it was, she would have already done it.

As it was, her stomach was tied into knots and her palms were so slick, she kept having to wipe them on her jeans one by one as she drove.

An hour into their trip, Jon asked, "Are you all right?"

Was she?

No.

But she was hoping she would be soon.

"I need to stop at a store coming up here." She nodded toward the backseat. "You wouldn't happen to have a ball cap in there, would you?"

"Ball cap?"

"Something I can hide my hair under."

He grabbed the duffel and put it between his knees. After a few moments, he pulled out a camo cap.

She smiled. "That'll do. Hold the wheel."

He did.

She twisted her hair up into a bun then fastened the hat down, so it was almost impossible to tell what color it was or how much of it she had.

"How's that?"

She looked to find him staring at her.

"What?"

He shook his head. "Nothing." He cleared his throat and then glared out the window. "Looks fine. Does the trick."

She smiled to herself.

"What do you need from the store?"

"Oh, I don't know. Serrated knife, duct tape and garbage bags for a start."

He stared at her.

"Just joking. Sort of." She shrugged. "A change of clothes might be nice. And I'm thinking I should change my look. Where we're going…well, it's important they don't see me coming."

"And where are we going?"

"To visit a few old friends."

Her palms were so damp now, not even rubbing them on her jeans helped.

She hadn't been back to the compound for over a year. And she really didn't like the idea of going back there now. Especially considering what she was going back for. And that a number of her old "friends" had now officially entered "enemy" territory.

But she had to go back, whether she wanted to or not.

She only hoped not too much had changed in the time she'd been gone. She was counting on that.

But if they had...

She took a deep, shuddering breath, knowing exactly what she was up against...and not liking it one bit.

She glanced at Reece, wondering if it was wise to involve him. But while she hadn't considered going it anything but alone just yesterday, today, well, for reasons she didn't think it smart to explore just then, she felt better with him at her side.

At the very least, she should let him in on it; give him the choice. And she would. Just as soon as she crossed the next item off her list.

She only hoped he'd stay on board. And wouldn't stamp her as insane and try to cart her off to the closest federal agency for immediate turnover.

Good thing the department store was just up the road. She really needed a chance to get her nerves under control, partly so she wouldn't lose control when she did drop in on old friends who were now her new enemies, but mostly so she wouldn't tip her hand to Reece, who suddenly seemed to be watching her a little too closely for comfort.

13

SHE WAS NUTS.

That was the first thought that hit Jon's mind when Mara told him what she planned to do.

"You're certifiable," he said, after what seemed like a full five minutes of silence when she'd stopped talking.

They sat in the parking lot of an old-time gas station up the road from the store—the type that had the analog pumps and the only form of security was a shotgun behind the counter. She'd emerged from the superstore where she'd gone in to buy a change of clothes and other supplies wearing tan slacks and a top. But it was after she'd come out of the gas station's public bathroom around the back, after what had seemed like an inordinately long time, that he'd been the most shocked.

Her hair...

Surely she hadn't been in there long enough for that drastic a change.

She'd gone in a long-haired redhead. And come out a short-haired blonde…

He'd thought for a minute it was a wig. But when he couldn't help touching it to find out, he'd discovered it was one hundred percent real.

And she was hotter still. A brush of makeup and she could be a local news anchor…or really hot weather person.

Then he'd caught a peek of the tattoo on her back left bare from her shorter hairstyle and tank top and knew she was the same person.

Well, except it appeared she may have bleached a good many of her brain cells along with her hair.

"You can't seriously be considering going there?"

He was aware of the compound that sat just north of Tuba City. Everyone who lived in northern Arizona knew of it…if only so they could avoid it at all costs.

And if ignorant, average citizens knew enough to stay away, what would happen to Mara, who ranked as public enemy number one, and whose cutout they were likely using for target practice?

Lord only knew what they'd do when they got a clear shot of the real thing.

You only had to look at what had gone down at the Winslow sheriff's office to catch that. And there had only been two militia members after her.

The compound would have at least a hundred militants at any one time. All of them well trained and well armed.

Mara shrugged. "I'm dead serious."

"The key word being *dead*."

She stared at her half-eaten sub, apparently suddenly having difficulty swallowing. He wanted to tell her to eat up, it very well may be her last meal. But he kept it to himself. Obviously he'd made his point and then some.

It was midday and the heat rose up in visible waves from the hot asphalt around them. Mara had switched off the engine and they sat with the window and doors open. The inside of the car felt like a veritable furnace.

But was no hotter than the opposition they'd face on that compound.

He caught his use of the joint pronoun and cursed under his breath.

He certainly wasn't planning on going in there with her, was he? If she was insane, that would make him doubly so.

"Look," she said, rewrapping the rest of the sandwich and stashing it in the bag. She downed half a bottle of water. "I lived there for four years. I know my way around."

"I don't doubt that. I also don't doubt that they're aware of that, too, and have likely made appropriate changes."

She nodded. "Granted. But not enough that I can't navigate my way around. Here, let me show you what I have in mind...."

She ripped open one of the white paper bags that had held their food, smoothed it out on the seat between them then grabbed a pen from the sun visor.

Jon stared, barely registering much outside the shape of her wrists, the way she smelled and how hot it was getting as she drew a rugged map of the compound, then lightly wrote on top of that with ways it had changed before.

"Personnel quarters are here," she said, drawing a number of small boxes under a cloud of trees on the northwest corner of the property. "That's my target."

"Our."

Her chin jerked up.

Jon grimaced. There was that joint pronoun again.

"Are you sure you want to do this?" she asked.

He picked up her map, trying to commit what she'd outlined to memory, but he found it hard to ignore his inner voice telling him he should be looking for an alternative.

Hell, for her own sake, he should drag her to the Flagstaff district offices now and turn her over.

Her being locked up—innocent or not—was preferable to her being dead.

His disabled cell phone weighed heavily in his pocket. He could call Lazarus.

He nearly snorted. And tell them what, exactly?

"Hey, I'm out here with the fugitive I'm supposed to be bringing in for that hefty bounty? Anyway, she didn't do it and I'm now helping her. Any advice?"

Of course, Lincoln Williams, one of the original partners, was ex-FBI. And while the two of them hadn't become close during the Florida job, he got the impression he could go to him whenever he had a problem.

And, oh, boy, Houston, did he ever have a problem.

The trouble was he was afraid his problem came in the form of one sexy, crazy Mara Findlay.

"Reece?"

"Huh?"

He'd noticed she'd taken to calling him by his last name. Which was fine. A lot of guys in the service had done the same.

But it was somehow different coming off her pink tongue. Made him feel different.

Made him feel a bit like he was back in the army formulating a difficult plan.

He slid his gun out of its holster. "We're going to need a hell of a lot more than just this and those play knives you picked up at the store before I'll even consider going in there."

Her smile melted into a full-out grin that did funny things to his stomach.

"Okay then. Let's see what we can do about that...."

MARA KNEW OF TWO OFF-COMPOUND sites where her old friends stashed their arms in case the main compound was ever "invaded" by local or federal authorities—something that had happened on at least one prior occasion. In fact, it had been because of that raid that they'd decided to split up the cache so they wouldn't be wiped out again, as they had been then. The raid had occurred before she'd ever met Gerald Butler when she was sixteen and fallen for him and his "family."

But while there were two sites, only one was open to her. And she counted herself lucky that the key operator was a true friend to her. Well, if he still held the position. And if he hadn't been turned against her.

Stop it, she ordered herself. Negative thinking never got anyone anywhere.

Then again, smart thinking was what had kept her alive this far.

"Okay, we're almost there," she said to Reece. "I want you to hang back a little and stay quiet, okay?"

His eyes narrowed.

"Just follow my lead."

She could tell that suggestion didn't sit well with him. Not that she could blame him. But the fact that he was still doing it? Well, his sticking by her despite his obvious doubts and concerns snuck by her defenses and took up residence somewhere in the vicinity of her chest.

She pulled onto what looked like a gravel road but was really a driveway. They drove for five minutes before a small shack came into view. It could have easily passed for a utility box, but she knew it wasn't. She also knew what was hidden inside.

She pulled to a stop and shut off the engine. She looked at Reece, who was taking in his surroundings. "My lead. Right?"

"Your lead," Reece confirmed.

"Leave your gun and holster here."

He hesitated.

She lifted a brow.

He did as she asked.

She climbed out of the SUV and raised her hands. "Trent? It's Mara."

Out of the corner of her eye, she saw Reece getting out with his hands up as well, moving slowly. He met up with her in front of the vehicle where they stood a couple of feet apart. She eyed the small camera perched on top of a pole above the shack, shifting to watch their every move.

"Stop there." A voice came through a speaker.

They did.

"Who's the mug?"

Mara nearly sagged in relief. This was definitely Trent.

She hadn't been sure what would go down if someone else had been assigned the post.

"A friend," she said.

"He looks like a cop."

"Don't we all?"

A laugh.

A moment later, the shed door opened and a lanky nineteen-year-old came loping out, his short-cropped red hair, freckles and infectious grin unchanged since the last time she'd seen him. He came to stand in front of her and she threw her arms around his tall frame.

"Hey, kiddo, how goes it?"

"One thing about the desert—it doesn't change," he said, awkwardly returning her hug.

"It changes you." She finished the sentence.

She stepped back.

"You look none the worse for wear."

"I'd say the same of you, but it wouldn't be true. What's with the hair?"

"I take it you've been out of touch for a while."

"They keep me blind and stupid. You know that."

She smiled. "Yeah. Long story. Anyway, I think I make a great blonde. Don't you?"

"I prefer you with black hair."

"Blond is my natural color."

"I know. But I prefer black." He openly stared at Reece, who'd dropped his hands, but was obviously being careful not to look like a threat.

"Trent, I want you to meet Reece. Reece, this is Trent."

Reece held out his hand. It looked for a moment like Trent wouldn't take it. Then when any other man might have rescinded the offer, the kid finally gave his hand a brief shake.

"I'm guessing your visit has nothing to do with pleasure," he said, turning his attention back to Mara.

"Oh, I don't know. Depends on your definition of pleasure…."

14

THE KID WAS CRUSHING on Mara so hard, Jon was surprised he wasn't drooling. As she requested, he hung back, which gave him a chance to watch the two interact. If he hadn't known Trent was involved in the militia, he would never have put him there, which is probably what made him a valuable asset. He looked as though he should be on his mom's couch somewhere, playing video games and snacking on chips with piles of comic books around him.

Funny thing was, Jon could still imagine him doing all that…only in a militia bunker, as isolated there as he would be at a parent's home.

Of course right that moment he was little more than a smart, attention-hungry puppy, running around Mara's ankles and licking her hands when he could reach them, even though his movements were slow and sluggish as if he wasn't getting enough to eat.

"Judge Judy?" Mara asked.

"People's Court."

"Eight minutes to Judge Whompner."

"What?"

Trent missed the *Rain Man* movie reference, but Jon got it and smiled.

Mara tsked. "You need to switch to the movie channels every now and again, kiddo."

"Yeah, well, they canceled those. I only get basic stations now. It sucks, 'cause I was getting into *Spartacus*."

"Seeing as they stuck you out here in the middle of nowhere by yourself, they could at least make sure you had premium channels."

"I know, right." They had begun walking toward the shack. "So what brings you out this way, Mara?"

Jon naturally tensed at the question, feeling more than a bit naked without his gun. While the kid appeared harmless enough, with everything going on, he would prefer to be prepared for anything just the same.

Mara leaned closer to Trent as they walked a few feet ahead of him. He couldn't make out what she said.

The kid stopped walking and stared off into the distance when she finished.

He had to give Mara credit. Rather than continue to try to convince Trent of whatever she'd asked of him, she merely stood waiting him out. Not many people were good at that art.

"I don't know, Mara," the kid finally said. "It could be my ass if they find out."

"They won't. Besides, it will be my ass if you turn me away."

Trent looked at her for a long moment.

"Okay."

Jon blinked. Although he agreed a world without Mara's fine ass in it would be a sad place, indeed, he wasn't sure he'd have agreed so readily.

He rubbed his chin and stared back at the SUV. What was he talking about? His position wasn't that far removed from Trent's.

Mara glanced over her shoulder at him, smiling. He was taken aback for a moment, then returned the smile. She nodded for him to follow.

She and Trent led the way about a hundred yards out in the shadow of a bluff. Then she and the kid began kicking around in the sand. He stood off to the side as Mara found a thick chain, the links of which measured about three inches wide, then Trent found another. Both of them rolled their chains around their shoulders then began walking away from the bluff with some effort. Slowly, the sand shifted and a large steel sheet slid open, revealing an entryway to an underground storage room.

Trent dropped the chain. "I just inventoried the ammo the other day. You should be able to take a few boxes without raising any brows."

Mara hugged him again. Strangely, Jon couldn't help but feel a brief sting of jealousy. The goofy way the kid grinned, it was as if she'd just given him the mother of all puppy treats.

He gave an eye roll, directed more at himself than anyone else, and followed when Mara motioned for him.

The gritty sand that had fallen when the top was open crunched underfoot as he descended the stairs behind her. The room was dark without a direct source of sunlight. Then Mara pulled a chain off to the side.

Holy shit.

"Holy shit," he said aloud.

Did he say *room?* The underground area looked more like it was the size of her warehouse…and was stacked to the ceiling with every firearm imaginable.

"Think any of these will do?" she asked, coming to stand next to him.

Jon picked up an old Winchester from a shelf and admired its well-oiled patina. He'd never seen one of these up close and personal, but he was pretty sure this was an 1873 First Model, better known as The Gun That Won The West.

Oh, yes. A few of these were going to do just fine. Not for the fight, but he was taking it nonetheless.

MARA WAVED THROUGH THE OPEN Blazer window as she drove away from Trent and his deceptive shack. She looked over to find Reece strapping his holster and gun back on, the expression on his face beyond amusing.

"Are you okay?" she asked.

"What? Oh, yeah." He ran his hand over his hair. She guessed it was maybe ten minutes or so into their "shopping" expedition that the light in his eyes had turned from "kid on Christmas morning" to "damn, this is some serious shit." He'd been helpful in getting the arms out to stash in the back of the car, catching Trent when he tripped on the chain and nearly fell, his arms filled with boxes of ammo. Mara had smiled at the automatic action.

Yes, Reece was a good egg.

She found herself wishing they had time to stop somewhere between there and the compound.

What was she talking about? She did have the time....

"I knew these guys were well armed," Reece said quietly. "I just had no idea how well armed. There's enough in that room to defend the entire country. Country? Five of them..."

She drove for ten minutes, then pulled off the main road again, heading up to the base of a butte, the idea in her head taking root and refusing to budge.

"What are we doing now?" he asked.

As soon as they were in the shadow of the butte, she rolled down the windows, shut off the engine and then climbed so she was straddling his hips on the bench seat.

He looked at her as if he couldn't have been more surprised had she dropped a rattlesnake in his lap.

"We're doing this..." she said, then leaned in to kiss him.

HOLY SHIT...

Those seemed to be the words of the hour, Jon noted as Mara kissed him.

Of all the things she could have chosen to do, this would have been the last thing he expected.

And he wasn't sure how he felt about it.

They'd just come from an arms munitions site the military would have killed to have, and were heading toward what might end up being The Last Stand at the OK Corral. And she wanted to fool around.

She squeezed his hips between her knees and rubbed her pelvis against a certain, traitorous part of his anatomy that was always up for anything she had in mind. Key word being *up*.

She was nuts.

She was also hotter than the Arizona desert.

He groaned, giving himself over to the emotions she was drawing out.

Good God in heaven, this bobcat was going to be the death of him.

That wouldn't bother him so much if he wasn't just a little bit afraid that it might be true.

He lifted his hands to frame her face and pulled her back a bit to look at her.

Damn, but the blond short cut was sexy as hell. The way a lock swooped down over her right brow brought out the green in her hazel eyes and, just as the slicked-back wet look had done the night before, further emphasized the plumpness of her lips.

"Did you really pull off to the side of the road to make out?" he asked.

Her mouth quirked upward. "Mmm-hmm... Any objections?"

She curved her hand over the bulge in the front of his jeans. He pressed against her shameless touch. "Not anymore."

She laughed then kissed him again. And again.

His physical desire for her outpaced even that from last night, if that was at all possible. Within minutes, they were both breathless and restless. She clawed at his T-shirt, ripping it off, and he did the same with her tank. He went to work on her jeans, and she did the same with his.

Finally they were stripped down and naked in the front of the Blazer.

Hell, he couldn't even remember doing this as a teen at midnight, yet here he was with Mara in the middle of the day, hungrier for her than any man had a right to be.

She straddled him again, kissing him senseless, then leaned back and reached between them, sheathing him with the condom she'd taken from his pocket then placing him against her. She waited for a heartbeat, biting slightly on her bottom lip, then she slid down over him, slowly, taking him in, inch by sweet inch, her lashes fluttering closed and a soft sound emerging from deep in her throat.

Jon grasped her hips, holding her still for a long moment. Had there ever been a hotter sight?

15

It normally took Mara a good long time to work up to this state of arousal and she and Reece had just begun.

There was something about him, about them together, that put her instantly outside herself, open to sensations and emotions she'd normally have to work at to achieve.

She rocked her hips, feeling red-hot ribbons of desire unfurl throughout her body.

Yes...

A part of her brain that still functioned told her the urgency of their situation might be partly to blame. When faced with the threat of death at every turn, enemies all around, things tended to emerge simpler than they did in everyday life.

Now...

Well, now, right now, nothing else mattered. There was only her. Him. Their joining.

"Damn," he whispered in her ear. "I need you to stop moving for a second."

Mara was tempted to ignore him. She knew he was close to the edge and wanted to push him into a free fall. But she wanted this to last.

She reluctantly slid off him, resting her temple against his, breathing in the masculine scent of his skin.

"Here, let's move to the back," he said, gesturing toward the back seat.

Without hesitation, she climbed over the bench and he followed. Before she could sit upright, he glided over her, pressing her against the cool leather and kissing her deeply.

Mara curved upward into him...against him, even as he nudged her knees apart and eased between her thighs.

He reentered her in one, smooth stroke.

Her back arched and she clutched his arms as if to steady herself although she was already anchored.

"God, you're so beautiful," he whispered into her ear, nuzzling the rim with his nose. "I don't ever want this to end."

Her spine melted, her every molecule responding to him physically and emotionally.

He moved and she moved with him, stroking, caressing, sighing, moaning. Then he was withdrawing again and turning her over, easing her up onto all fours, his front plastered against her back. She felt his hand against her tattoo, drawing firm lines over it, then smoothing his palm across the width of it.

Mara reached over to draw his head closer to hers, kissing him over her shoulder.

His fingers budged from where they were pressed against her trembling stomach, traveling up to pluck her nipples, then drifting down, and down farther yet, his thumb parting her, pressing against her clit. She gasped and he thrust into her, chasing out whatever little breath remained in her lungs.

No... she wanted to say. Not yet.

Not yet...

Even as she thought the words, her body betrayed her, swirling tremors beginning at her core and growing ever wider, until she couldn't think, couldn't move, could do no more than surrender to the overwhelming sensations.

"I'm coming," Reece said through his teeth, grasping her hips tightly.

"I'm already there...."

JON WATCHED AS THE SUN began its slow descent toward the horizon from where he leaned against the side of the SUV, noting the way the bright orange orb appeared to grow in size, a trick of the atmosphere, pollution.

He glanced through the open window at where Mara still slumbered in the backseat. He'd draped a T-shirt he'd fished from his duffel over her, but she'd shifted so it barely covered her waist and breasts.

He experienced a wave of protectiveness wash over him.

Ironic that the first woman he'd felt that way about was probably the last one who needed it?

He squinted into the sunset, considering everything that had happened over the past two days, then took a drink from one of the iced water bottles Mara had bought at the market. He wanted to access his cell phone, but didn't dare, and actually, in an odd way he couldn't quite explain, he felt better, more focused without it.

He heard rustling behind him and turned to find Mara stirring.

She blinked open her eyes, lifted her head and looked around.

"Hey," he said.

She met his gaze and smiled. "Hey, yourself." She yawned then looked beyond him toward the sunset. The smile disappeared, seeming to take the warmth with it.

"Almost time," he said.

He could virtually hear the sand pouring out of the hourglass; he only hoped it represented the minutes of the day and not anything more significant.

Mara sat up, collected her clothes from where he'd laid them on the back of the seat and began getting dressed. "I'm thinking maybe we have an hour... maybe less."

"I'm thinking you're right."

She finished pulling on her boots and fixing her hair in the rearview mirror. "Are you sure you're up for this?"

Was she asking him if he wanted to reconsider? Back out?

Yes, he realized, she was.

"I'm certainly not letting you go in there without me," he said.

"That doesn't answer my question."

"I'm positive."

He held her gaze for as long as it took to convey his feelings. When she looked away, he opened the door and handed her the water bottle. She took a long sip.

"How far away are we?" he asked.

"Twenty minutes. I didn't want to come in too close in case someone from the compound spotted me," she said. "They're all over."

He nodded. "I figured as much." He looked back out at the sunset. "Is it okay if we make a stop first?"

"Sure. Where?"

He glanced back at her. "My mom's place."

MARA DIDN'T QUITE KNOW how to respond.

"She's not far from here," he said. "And it wouldn't be for long."

Was it her or did he look almost shy?

"I figured since we were out this way, I should drop in and say hi. She'd kill me if she found out I was nearby and didn't come home."

She couldn't help smiling at that.

Her mother wouldn't have thought anything of her being a block away and not stopping in. In fact, Tatiana would probably be a little chilly if Mara didn't

give her at least a week's notice. Unexpected visits
messed with her chakras, she said, and interfered with
her creativity, which in recent years was with clay.
Mara had learned the hard way, as the only child of
a single mother, that you never wanted to mess with
Mom's chakras.

She supposed it was one reason why she'd loved
spending time with her dad. Although her parents had
never married—and she was a result of a brief affair
while her dad was home on leave—he'd always been a
great father, picking her up the instant he was in town
and keeping her until it was time to go, making her a
priority and playing the role of daddy as dedicatedly
as he did that of solider.

He'd remarried when she was ten and had given her
a brother and a sister with whom she shared a close
bond. Since her father had died, and her stepmother
remarried, however, she didn't see her much younger
siblings as much as she'd like, only around the holi-
days and their birthdays. But they were her blood and
she loved them.

And she liked knowing there were more parts of
her dad living and breathing out there that were also
a part of her.

She finished off the water then wiped her palms
on her jeans. She couldn't help getting the impression
Reece wanted to see his mother in case something
happened and…

And, well, maybe he'd never see her again.

She shuddered at the idea and searched for wood

to knock on, an old tradition she'd learned from her father, who had been interestingly superstitious as well as a huge romantic, in spite of his chosen career.

She realized she hadn't answered Reece and he was looking at her curiously.

"Would you like to drop me somewhere and go yourself?" she asked.

He blinked as if the thought hadn't occurred to him. "No. No...I'd..."

She waited.

"I'd like her to meet you...."

His quiet words made her heart double in size.

Reece looked down at his dusty boots and grinned. "I can't promise there won't be questions, though. Some of them may be awkward."

Mara laughed. "Awkward's my middle name. Or haven't you figured that out yet?"

His gaze met hers and she nearly lost her breath.

If you'd have asked her just a day ago if she'd ever known love, she'd have told you yes, she had.

But in that one moment, merely looking at Reece, and having him looking at her, she knew a connection that transcended any she'd ever experienced. And it made her wonder if, in fact, she'd ever known love at all....

16

BETTINA MACINTIRE REECE had been an elementary school nurse when she'd met her husband-to-be over thirty years ago. And while Jon suspected most women were natural nurturers, his mother...well, when he'd compared her to others while growing up, he knew she surpassed most if not all of them.

Even now, years after his father had passed, she continued on as if she expected him to come home any minute.

For simplicity's sake, Mara had turned the driving over to him. And now as he pulled up the long drive-way leading to the house he'd grown up in, he couldn't help noticing the little touches that had always made the house a home.

The four-bedroom hacienda–type one-story struc-ture flowed one room into the next, each airier than the one before with windows either looking out over the desert landscape or over the interior courtyard with a water fountain his father had built for his mother's birthday one year, flowers blooming year-round.

He and his siblings had grown up there, and his bedroom was still his.

With a bit of nostalgia, he realized when he thought of being home, this had always been it. Everywhere else he'd lived had only been a place to catch some sleep and stow his stuff, up to and including the rental house he currently shared with Julie.

"This is it," he said unnecessarily, since turning off the road made that obvious.

No response.

He glanced at Mara. She plucked and worried over her appearance in the dusty visor mirror. He pulled to a stop beside an unfamiliar Cadillac near the four-car garage around the back of the main house and switched off the engine.

He didn't think he'd ever seen her nervous before. But he was pretty sure that's what was behind her messing with her hair for the fifth time since he'd begun driving the short distance to his mother's place. She'd also applied makeup, only to wipe half of it off moments later.

Had Julie been nervous about meeting his mother? He tried to recall. Then he realized, no, she hadn't. She'd been complaining about the flight delay they'd encountered and how she planned to file a complaint as soon as they settled in. He'd lightly told her the airline had no control over the weather—they'd encountered severe thunderstorms—but she hadn't been deterred and was insistent she at least be given a complimentary ticket to make up for her inconvenience.

Odd, he'd never really noticed until then that she'd never really referred to them as "we" or "us." It was always her...and him as an afterthought.

How strange was that?

"Don't worry. She's going to love you," he said to Mara.

She blinked at him, looking pale. "How do you know that?"

He was intrigued that his mother's liking her meant something to her. Somehow, he more likely would have expected her to tap her watch and say the clock was ticking. If ever a woman had cause to do exactly that, it was Mara. After all, it wasn't as if she had an important sale to catch, or a manicurist appointment to make.

He wondered at her many facets. Would he ever reach a point where he wouldn't marvel at each as it was revealed?

The thought caught him up short. Still, he grinned at her reassuringly. "While I'd like to say it's because you're lovable—" that earned him a saucy shadow of a smile "—the fact is, my mother's one of those irritating types who loves everybody."

"Ah," she said, her gaze darting around.

He questioned whether she'd heard his response at all or if he'd lost her to whatever was going on inside that pretty head of hers again.

"Come on," he said. "She prides herself on her

coffee and I have to say it's some of the best. Okay, it *is* the best."

He climbed out of the Blazer and stood next to the front bumper, staring at the Caddy as he waited for her to join him. He was curious as to why his mom hadn't come out yet. Usually she'd have been at the side of the car before he could shut off the engine.

"Nice place," Mara said, walking with him to the back door. "This where you grow up?"

"Yeah. Me and my two brothers and sister."

"Bet it was great."

He agreed. "It was."

She stopped walking. "Shit. We should have stopped for something."

"How do you mean?"

"It's bad etiquette to show up empty handed. Not to mention bad luck."

"This isn't exactly your run-of-the-mill visit, Mara," he said softly.

"For us, no. But it is for her."

There was still no sign of his mother. Was she maybe not home? He couldn't imagine where she'd be at this time of day.

He took out his keys and opened the back door for Mara to enter, then followed.

The kitchen was painted in yellows and browns with Spanish tiles and it smelled of *menudo*. He stepped to the stove and lifted a lid.

Yes...

"Jonny!"

He turned to find his mother standing in the kitchen doorway wearing a short pink silk robe, her hair mussed, her lipstick smeared.

Never had he seen her in something so...revealing. Her robes had always been made of thick terry cloth and covered her ankles. That's when he'd seen her in them, which had been rarely and even then, only in the morning, not this early in the evening.

She barely looked like his mother at all.

Then what he guessed to be the owner of the Cadillac stepped up behind her wearing nothing but a towel draped around his hips: a man of about his mother's age with salt-and-pepper hair and tanned skin.

Jon stared as if the contents of the pan had been dumped over his head....

"OH, THIS IS AWKWARD," the man standing behind what Mara gathered was Reece's mother said, trying to smooth his hair.

She hid a small smile. It was obvious to anyone paying attention what the two had been doing, and it wasn't gardening.

It was also obvious that Reece couldn't have been more shocked had someone told him he was a love child and his father had been the milkman.

"What are you doing here?" his mother said, rushing into the room to hug him.

Reece returned the hug, but half-heartedly. His gaze was fixed on the man still standing in the doorway.

"I, um, will leave you alone for a moment." The man backed into the other room, then disappeared.

"I didn't know you were going to be in town," his mother said. "You should have called."

"I didn't realize I had to."

Silence fell.

His mother finally seemed to catch on that there was someone else in the room. She turned to look at Mara, blinking.

"Hi," Mara said, extending her hand. "Sorry to be a bother. We were in the neighborhood, so to speak, and Reece thought it would be nice to drop by."

"Oh, yes. Of course," his mother said. "And your name?"

"I'm sorry. Mara. My name is Mara."

"Nice to meet you, Mara."

"Nice to meet you, as well, Mrs. Reece."

Silence fell again.

Mara could tell Reece was having a hard time formulating something to say. And, for the life of her, she couldn't come up with anything, either. At least not something that wasn't entirely lame.

"You have a very nice home, Mrs. Reece," she said, giving in to the urge to voice one of the more forgiving comments.

"Thank you. Thank you very much. And it's Bettina. Please…"

Mara cleared her throat, waiting for Reece to snap out of it.

"Um, I'm just going to go check…" Mrs. Reece

said, gesturing over her shoulder at the now empty doorway. "I'll be right back."

She couldn't have hurried out of the room faster if she'd run.

Mara tucked her chin into her chest, trying to muffle her laugh.

Reece still stared after where his mother had been.

"Oh, this is awkward," she said quietly, echoing the visitor's reaction.

Reece looked at her. "I… She…"

Mara cleared her throat and smiled widely.

Finally the ice seemed to crack on his face. "What in the hell was that?"

He laughed and she joined him.

"I'm guessing that's the first time you've seen your mother with someone who was not your father?"

"Are you kidding? That's the first time I've seen my mother like that even with my father."

"Well. It seems you're not the only one capable of surprises."

Reece didn't appear to hear her. "She's throwing a fiftieth wedding anniversary party for the family next month."

Mara blinked. "To honor her wedding to your dad?"

He nodded.

"I wonder if she planned to introduce her new beau at the event."

Reece wasn't amused.

She cleared her throat. "Sorry."

He began pacing back and forth, amusing her further, although she didn't think it was a good idea to let him know that. He genuinely looked like a six-year-old kid who'd just found out there was no Santa Claus.

"She is human, Reece," she said quietly. "And a relatively young and attractive one at that."

He stared at her as if she were speaking a foreign language.

"What upsets you more? That she's not remaining forever faithful to your father's memory?" she asked. "Or that she's not remaining faithful to your idea of her as your mother?"

He stopped and leaned his hands against the tiled island. "Not fair."

"Maybe. Maybe not."

He looked at her for a long few moments and then pushed away. "I need some coffee. You want some?"

"I thought you'd never ask...."

17

JON WAS STILL TRYING to process everything when his mother came back into the room looking like she usually did in light-colored jeans and white blouse. She easily nudged him out of the way and made the coffee, taking three cups out of the cupboard and talking about the weather and the new shrubs she'd planted along the back of the property line. For a moment, it was all too easy to forget what had happened a few minutes ago.

Until her "friend" popped back up into the kitchen doorway, also dressed and cleaned up.

"Oh, there you are, Joe," she said as if she'd just opened the back door to find him standing there, a neighbor or old friend. "Come in, come in. I'd like you to meet my middle child, Jonathon. Jonny, this is Joe Winters. He just bought the old Branson ranch up the road."

Joe crossed the room and extended his hand, looking friendly enough. The problem was, he looked a little *too* friendly.

Mara had come to stand next to Jon and she nudged him with her elbow now.

He shook Joe's hand.

"Nice to meet you, Jon," the older man said. "Your mom speaks of you often."

"Funny. She's never mentioned you."

There was a clatter from his mom's direction at the sink as she dropped something.

"I hear you work out of Colorado Springs?" Joe said smoothly. "High-risk private security company?"

He nodded. "Yeah."

"Join us for coffee, Joe?" his mother asked.

"No, no, thank you. None for me." He smiled that too-friendly smile at her. Jon didn't like it. "I really hate to meet and run, but truth is, I'm needed back at the ranch."

"Oh?" Jon said. "It hasn't been a running ranch for nearly a decade."

"Jonny!" his mother said.

"It's okay, Betti." Joe looked back at him. "I've been busy for the past six months getting it back up and running."

Six months. He'd been there for six months.

How much of that time had he spent banging his mother? Or, pardon, Betti.

Not even his father had called her Betti.

How much did his brothers and sister know about this?

And if they did know, why in the hell hadn't anyone told him? It might have saved them all an awkward moment.

God, would he ever be able to just walk into the place again?

His mother handed Mara a cup of coffee, then thrust one out in front of him. He took it.

"I'll walk you out, Joe," she said.

"Oh, no need to run on account of me," Jon said, now wanting to know more where seconds before, he hadn't wanted to know anything.

"I'm not, son. It's just time for me to go is all." He extended his hand again. "Nice meeting you. Hope to see you again soon."

Don't count on it, Jon thought. *And I'm not your son.*

He watched as his mother went to open the door, glaring at him in the same way she had when he was a kid and he'd cracked on some of the parishioners during mass.

Joe said goodbye to Mara and then walked outside, Jon's mom following.

Mara burst out laughing as soon as the door was closed.

"What?" he demanded. What could she possibly find amusing about this situation. There was nothing amusing about it.

She stopped laughing but obviously with some effort. "Nothing. It's just that…"

"What?"

"Well, if that wasn't a pissing match and a half, I don't know what is."

He set his back teeth together. "I haven't a clue what you're talking about."

"Oh, I think you know exactly what I'm talking about."

He heard the Caddy start.

A Caddy.

His dad had always favored trucks and SUVs. Something more manly.

"Right now, you're about as clear as a mud puddle," he told Mara.

"You and Joe. As far as I'm concerned, you might as well have whipped them out right here in front of me and your mother."

The door opened and whatever response he would have made stuck to his tongue as if superglued.

She made another comment about the weather, the heat and what it meant to her water bill as she went to the kitchen table with her coffee, indicating they should follow her.

Jon reluctantly did, but he watched as Mara hung back a moment before saying, "Mrs. Reece, you do have a such a beautiful house. And I spotted that courtyard. Do you mind if I have a look around?"

His mother started to get up. "Not at all, dear. Let me—"

"No, no, that's not necessary. You two stay here and, um, talk. I can take care of myself. I'll just be out in the courtyard if you need me."

Jon squinted at her, then realized what she was doing. She was giving them space in order to have this thing out.

"Very well," his mother said. "Here, why don't you take your coffee with you?"

"Thanks. I think I will." She lifted the mug from the kitchen table. "Reece said yours was the best. I have to say, I agree."

Then she wandered off, leaving him alone with his mother.

EVERY NOW AND AGAIN, Mara glimpsed mother and son through the interior windows. She hadn't lied; the place was beautiful. Exactly the type of house she had once dreamed about living in when she was younger. Then she woke up and realized her chances of ever staying in such a place, much less living in one, were virtually nil. Not with her wandering mother and career military father.

It wasn't that the place was expensive. No, that's not what she meant. It was just…

A home.

Something she'd really never known.

She glanced in Reece's direction again. At first, it appeared that he and his mother were attempting to keep up the front that all was okay. But she knew the instant it collapsed to rubble when Mrs. Reece's back went up and Jon leaned forward in accusatory animation. She could virtually hear him saying something along the lines of, "How could you?"

Then Mrs. Reece said something that knocked him back on his heels.

She smiled at their obvious closeness, then turned to appreciate the flowers and plants around the courtyard. She didn't know what was being said. She didn't have to know. The fact that they were seated at a kitchen table working it out…wow! While she'd had that kind of relationship with her father, well, it hadn't really factored much into her life outside those brief patches. Her mother was quick to respond and long to change her mind. Which meant there had been long silences in between. It had started when she was five and had slammed the door on one of her mother's boyfriends—before she'd enlarged her dating pool to include women—telling him they didn't want him there and never to come back.

Her mother had made her suffer for a week of silence that time.

It probably hadn't been the first time. But it was the first time she remembered. And it had killed her.

Mara attempted to shrug off the unwanted emotion, not wanting to go where those journeys ultimately led her.

Too late.

Within a blink of an eye, she was sixteen again, standing in the small, useless kitchen of her mother's apartment—funny, that's how she'd always viewed each successive place they lived in, always her mother's, never hers. None of the appliances had worked, including the refrigerator, so she'd regularly been required to go get ice in order to keep the interior cold.

"I'm moving on," her mother had said following a ten-day silence, punishment for Mara's skipping school with a girlfriend and hanging out on the lush green of a golf course soaking up the spring sun.

She'd merely stared at her mother, trying to grasp what she was saying.

"I have an opportunity to travel with a friend to Baja. And I'm going to take it."

And just like that, Mara had been left without a home.

"Where am I supposed to go?" she'd asked, hating the words as she said them, hating her weakness, hating her remaining parent's lack of concern for her only child.

Her mother had shrugged as she went to the bedroom closet and collected the box of her things she always kept packed. It had gotten smaller, rather than bigger, over the years and contained nothing of Mara's that she could tell. "You have three days to figure it out. Maybe your stepmother will take you in. Wherever you end up, I'm sure you'll be fine. I was on my own at your age. And I don't think I turned out so badly."

The next day she'd met Gerald Butler. And the militia had become her home and family.

"Mara?"

She blinked from where she'd been fingering a

cactus, not realizing she was bleeding until Reece had said her name.

She squeezed her fingers into her palm and looked up at him.

"Are you okay?"

At the look of concern on his handsome face, the shadows instantly fled.

"I am now," she whispered, too low for him to hear.

Jon STILL WASN'T SURE what Mara had been thinking about when he found her in the courtyard, but he did know he hadn't liked it.

She'd looked so…lost. So very alone.

"So, is everything okay?" she asked.

He stared at her, trying to make sense out of her words.

"Between you and your mother? Are you two working everything out?"

He grimaced.

"*Working* being the operative word."

He still didn't know what to make of what had happened earlier. Bettina Reece had never been anything short of the perfect housewife and mother. To see her mussed up like that, obviously having just come from bed…

He grimaced again, hoping to erase that particular memory from his mind as quickly as he could.

"Julie's been calling here," his mother had told him, once he was finished unloading on her about her activities.

Julie.

It seemed they both had some explaining to do.

Thankfully that part of his relationship with his mother hadn't changed; he could still talk to her about anything.

"I've been seeing Joe since about the day he took possession of the ranch," she'd admitted to him. "Trust me, it's the last thing I was looking for. I'd planned to stay alone for the rest of my life. After your father…"

She'd drifted off, the pained expression on her face hitting him hard.

He'd then realized what an ass he was being and grudgingly apologized. He admitted it had been a shock seeing her and Joe. And, yeah, a childish part of him wished things could stay the same. But she looked happier than he'd seen her in a long, long while. And if Joe was responsible for that? Well, the least he could do was call in advance when he was going to visit.

Then his mom asked about Mara. And he'd been reluctant to tell her the truth of the situation. So he'd merely said she was a friend.

His mother had smiled at him in the same way she had when she'd found out that he'd gotten that skinned chin from climbing into the attic of the garage to get at his grandfather's war medals, a place he wasn't supposed to be.

As he looked at Mara now, he wondered if a skinned chin was all he would come away with.

"Come on. Let's get your hand taken care of, finish coffee with my mom and get this thing done."

She stared at her fingers as if only noticing the blood now, then smiled at him. "Let's do it...."

18

MARA FOUND IT IRONIC that in a matter of hours, they would visit both Reece's home, and the only home she had ever known.

Of course, they were miles apart, and not only in distance. Shoot her, but she didn't think any of Reece's family members would ever try to kill him.

"Whoa." Reece leaned over to correct the wheel where she'd accidentally driven over the line and onto the right shoulder.

Damn.

The sun had long since set, taking with it the power to chase away shadows. They needed darkness in order to do what had to be done, but night was always the time when ghosts felt the closest. In this case, ghosts of relationships past.

Gerald Butler...

She gave a sad internal smile. How dynamic he had seemed when she first met him. Attentive. He'd seemed to fill all the holes in her life with ease, pulling her both to him and into the fold of the militia family when she'd needed him most. The compound was where she'd learned to live in harmony with others. There had been a certain symmetry to the lifestyle. A kind of commune, only with guns. They each were assigned their duties, and when the day was done, they gathered together around a fire to talk until they each drifted off to bed.

She understood now how very young she'd been. And because of her circumstances, so very vulnerable. But she had always believed Gerald had loved her, even though she had left when she was eighteen, served a brief stint in the military then lived pretty much solo ever since.

How stupid she'd been.

"Pull over."

She looked at Reece. "What?"

"I said pull over. Here. Now."

Thinking he'd seen something she hadn't, she searched her rearview and side mirrors. Had the FBI been watching his mother's house? Had they picked up their scent there and were tailing them?

She didn't see anything.

"Why?" she asked.

"Damn it, Mara, just pull over."

She did so, kicking up dust as the right wheels went over the side of the road into the desert sand. She pulled to a stop and the dust clouded around the Blazer, completely engulfing them.

As soon as it settled, Reece got out of the car. She got out, too.

"What's going on?" she asked, coming to stand next to him on the other side.

She found him staring off into the eastern horizon where a full moon was just beginning to rise.

"Reece?"

"Shhh…" he said.

She looked at him, the moon, then him again.

"Reece, what in the hell is—"

He took her by the arms and kissed her.

Mara gasped, shocked by the unexpected move.

He slid his mouth against hers, hotly. She resisted. This wasn't the time for making out. She had to finish this. Clear her name. Find a way to get back to familiar territory before no territory was ever familiar again.

The thought caught her off guard.

But Reece persisted, his attention all consuming.

Soon enough, she was responding to him against her own will. Opening her lips, welcoming his tongue…

Her backbone sighed and she surrendered to the moment, kissing him in the light of the full moon. Kissing him until not a thought remained in her head beyond him, right now, his mouth.

He slowly pulled away, then held her close.

She heard the thrum of his heartbeat beneath her ear. Felt the warm cotton of his T-shirt. Smelled his detergent and his skin.

She remembered earlier, when she'd turned off the

road and climbed on top of him, needing him on a physical level she hadn't been able to ignore.

Was that what this was about?

"I needed to wipe that look from your face," he said quietly into her ear, his fingers caressing her scalp where they'd tunneled through her hair.

"I don't understand."

He pulled back to gaze down at her. "Mara, I...I can't imagine what must be going through your mind now...or what you were thinking back at the house when you pricked your hand on that cactus. But whatever it is, you need to find a way to get a handle on it...."

She looked away, unable to meet his gaze. Was she really that transparent?

She tried to move away, but he prevented it.

"I think we should postpone this," he said.

"What? No way."

He set her on her feet away from him, still gently but firmly holding her upper arms. "Look, Mara, I can't think of anyone I'd rather go into a hostile situation with...when you're operating on all twelve cylinders. Right now, well, you're distracted."

"I'm not distracted."

He raised a brow. "Oh? Then you meant to go off the road back there then? Is that what you're telling me?"

"I didn't go off the road. I merely veered a little onto the shoulder...."

She knew she was fighting a losing battle. He was right. She was distracted.

She drew in a deep breath and he released his grip. Then she took off into a dead run.

"What the hell?" he called after her.

"Be back in a half hour," she said. "A good run always helps me concentrate."

Within a blink he was next to her.

"What are you doing?"

"Running with you, of course. Now hush up and pick up the pace...."

FORTY-FIVE MINUTES LATER, they were back in the car and Mara was laser focused on what lay ahead.

They'd both cleaned up using the now warm bottles of water remaining. While they didn't want to smell like soap, they didn't want to reek, either. Any kind of overpowering scent might be enough to give them and their positions away, especially if there were dogs around. And complete secrecy and cover was a necessary component to the success of this mission.

Mission.

Yes. Given what they were about to do, and where they were about to do it, this very much resembled a military operation. They would be invading a well-armed, well-protected compound of which any small country would be proud. And there were only the two of them, with no backup, to do it.

She shivered.

At the store earlier, she'd picked up two short-range radios. They'd synced them to the same channel. While they didn't plan to be apart often, there was always a chance they'd get separated. And if they did, they needed to be able to communicate with each other.

She drew in a deep, calming breath. Yes, she was nervous. Her adrenaline was running high. But she was focused. Together.

A glance in Reece's direction told him he was the same.

She finally pulled off the road a mile away from the compound's southeastern perimeter and killed the engine. They sat in silence for a few moments, staring out at the relative darkness. Clouds skidded across the face of the full moon, dulling its brightness before moving on. She'd have preferred no moon, but there was no way she was putting this off any longer. It was only a matter of time before the FBI, militia goons or even another bounty hunter caught up with them. And then where would she be?

Exactly where Butler and his followers intended her to be—behind bars serving time for a crime she didn't commit.

Or worse, dead.

"Ready?" she asked, taking a shuddering breath.

"There."

She climbed out of the Blazer and he did, too. They checked their radios one last time, put on their bulletproof vests, fastened their ammo and gun belts, then stood looking at each other.

She leaned up and kissed him, briefly but fully.

"What was that for?"

She smiled. "Luck."

Then she set off on a moderate jog toward the compound, with him following close behind.

She knew where the compound cameras were located and which places to avoid, but there was always the possibility they'd updated their security system.

Before she knew it, they were at the perimeter and the electrified, razor wire fence. She watched as Reece worked to reroute the dangerously high voltage flow of electricity, leaving a stretch safe without setting off any alarms to the disruption. As soon as he gave the thumbs-up, she went to work cutting out an entry in the chain link large enough for them to get through.

Then they were inside.

Butler's personal quarters were about a half mile to the west. The closer they got, the denser security would get.

Thankfully, the compound was in northern Arizona and tree cover was plenty. The group leaders had reasoned that they couldn't be easily watched or tracked from the outside or above.

What it also meant was that she and Reece could move with some ease once inside, moving from pine to pine, keeping to the shadows, which were few due to massive security lighting.

A quarter of a mile in, she heard some conversation. She stopped and motioned to Reece, only he had already drawn to a halt. She listened for a minute, un-

familiar with the voices. She glanced toward the left.
Reece nodded and she led the way.

Another two minutes and they had Butler's quarters within eyeshot.

Okay.

Mara stopped to gain her bearings, mentally reviewing her plans.

Butler's quarters were made up of a small, one-bedroom cabin set well apart from other structures.
There wasn't another building or cabin for at least two hundred yards in any direction. He valued privacy above all else.

Butler wasn't there, of course; he was behind bars awaiting trial. But there was a light on in the place, indicating someone had taken up residence while he was away.

Damn.

She heard a dull thump.

She swiveled, her gun held at the ready to find Reece grinning at her fifteen feet away. He gestured downward. At his feet was one of the militia guards.
She remembered the guy well. He'd been the first to object to her inclusion in the "family" and watched her every move like a hawk. A very hungry one.

Criminy. She was thankful Reece had her back.

All right. This was where they were to part company. She was to make a move on Butler's cabin while Reece would provide cover. She sincerely hoped she didn't need it. There were at least a hundred militia members at any one time on the compound. While she and Reece were well armed, they weren't armed well enough to fight off that many unless they got a head start.

Well, then, they'd just have to make sure they got a head start, wouldn't they?

If they needed one at all.

Reece came to stand next to her and readied the heavier of his loaded weapons so they leaned against nearby pines within arm's reach. She did the same with two shotguns she would be leaving behind, although she was still strapped with four automatics and extra ammo.

She watched him take the bow he'd brought from over his arm and repositioned the quiver of arrows.

Mara took a deep breath. This was it.

She met his gaze and held it for long moments.

It seemed in that moment, she'd known him forever.

Yet a quiet internal voice whispered, *Please, I've just found you. Don't let me lose you now.*

She closed her eyes, took a deep breath then looked at him again, giving him a thumbs-up.

Then he did something that rocked her to the soles of her boots: he placed his finger against his pursed lips, then pressed them lightly against hers.

She smiled and he nodded, indicating it was time for her to go.

She readied herself to skirt the trees to the side of the cabin even as Reece took aim, his target a guard near where she planned to enter. She silently counted, watching as the man neared the tree line then began to turn around.

Whoosh!

Reece shot and the arrow caught the guy in the upper arm. The guard's hand automatically went to the offending object, but before he could pull it out, he dropped to his knees and then fell forward altogether as a result of the knockout agent Reece had applied to the tip.

She nodded at him.

Her turn.

She took off at a fast run.

Please, let this all go according to plan....

19

DAMN.

The instant Mara was out of eyeshot, Jon experienced his first dose of pure fear. So long as he could see her, he was okay. But now that he couldn't…

He wiped his brow on the long sleeve of his dark shirt. He'd traded his bow for a 20-gauge shotgun and was now training it on the cabin. He surveyed the area through the scope, switching to night vision to sweep the forest, as well.

Clear.

For now.

But he knew how quickly that could change.

He'd been in similar situations before. It went hand in hand with active service in a war zone. But every job was different, with variables you could plan for… and others you couldn't.

Despite the detailed map Mara had made for him of the compound, he'd already noted a few differences. Like the cameras. A few more had been added since she'd last been there. And another trail. That didn't concern him so much as what else might have been changed that they hadn't allowed for.

He'd noticed a light on in the cabin. It was entirely possible it had been taken over by someone else high up in the command. Maybe what she was after was no longer even there.

And if that was the case…

He glimpsed movement to the right of the cabin.

Damn.

He focused on the guard closing in. He gauged the distance between him and the downed guard on the opposite side to be forty feet. If he spotted him…

He couldn't chance live fire. Not yet. There wasn't enough time for Mara to have gained access to the cabin yet, much less get what she was after, which she'd said was in a locked safe.

He exchanged the shotgun for his bow and trained his sights on the guard moving ever closer to the downed one.

The moment his pace picked up, indicating he'd seen the other guy, he shot…and hit the man in the right shoulder.

He stumbled, but didn't fall and was reaching for his radio.

Jon reloaded and aimed again, hitting him in the other arm.

Bingo.

Down he went, right next to the other one.

He traded off for the shotgun again and swept the area with the scope, including behind him.

Come on, Mara. Come on...

MARA USED A GLASSCUTTER to create a hole large enough for her to reach in and unlock the window, then opened it and slid inside. The light wasn't on in the living area of the cabin; it was coming from the bedroom. Unfortunately, that was exactly where she needed to go.

She checked her radio, then moved to the bedroom door that was slightly ajar.

A young woman lay across the bed, talking on a cell phone.

Butler's latest girl, she had no doubt.

She wore an oversize man's T-shirt, likely belonging to him. Mara winced at the thought she had done exactly the same thing.

At least a glimpse around verified it was still Butler's cabin and not somebody else's. His personal belongings were still everywhere, his pictures on the wall.

She considered her options.

Since she didn't know who the woman was talking to, she didn't want to bust in and risk it was someone within the compounds, which wasn't too far of a stretch because once you were within the "family," nothing else existed.

She eyed the front door a few feet away then made her way toward it. Taking a deep breath, she knocked three times in quick succession then ducked back into the shadows beside the bedroom door.

She heard a heavy sigh. "Hold on, Jenna, there's somebody knocking." Bedsprings squeaked. "Probably one of those stupid guards again. I swear, sometimes I feel I have more to fear from them…"

She came outside the room.

In a split-second decision, Mara grabbed the woman's arm holding the cell phone then twisted it behind her, quickly bringing her other hand down over her mouth.

Within thirty seconds flat, she had her cuffed and locked in the closet, with tape over her mouth.

Butler was slipping. The women he chose usually had at least some skill. She would never have been such easy quarry.

Of course, none of that brought her any pleasure. In the end, they were all little more than temporary, expendable playthings.

She slipped inside the bedroom, took out dresser drawers then pulled the dresser itself back. She eyed the paneling, trying to remember how to access the door that hid the safe. She tried one way, then another with no luck.

"Screw it."

She took out the twelve-inch serrated knife from the sheath strapped to her leg and forced the paneling open.

Then she stood staring at a different safe than she'd expected to find.

Damn.

Damn, damn, damn.

She crouched down to get a closer look, ignoring the kicks to the closet door that began along with muffled shouts.

She noted that while the safe was different, it still had a combination lock.

She smiled.

If Butler stayed true to form...

She tried his mix of numbers from his birthday, his dad's birthday and the date he became "General."

Nothing.

Damn.

She sat down heavily, tears flooding her eyes.

What was she going to do now? This was her only hope of clearing her name. Papers inside the safe proved that the federal prosecutor she was accused of killing had close ties with the group. And that he had refused to show special favor when Butler had pulled strings and managed to get his case before him.

Moreover, these were also proof that the new prosecutor was in Butler's back pocket and had been for years.

Listlessly, she reached for the numbered knob again, hopelessly going through the numbers: 31-12-7.

She sat for long moments, her heart thudding loudly in her ears. Louder than the kicks to the closet door.

Her hand shaking, she reached for the handle...

It opened.

Thank you, thank you, thank you, thank you...

She opened the drawstring bag she'd brought along and started stuffing the appropriate folders inside, along with a few other items that might help her out. Or, at the very least, prevent her from finding herself in this predicament again.

Had she been thinking when she left years ago, she'd have done it then. So long as the group thought she had information that could bring them down stashed somewhere in the event something happened to her, she'd be safe.

Essentially, what was in the folders was a list of people with longtime ties to the group, ranging from local law enforcement to national politicians.

What would help free her now was the fact that the federal prosecutor who would replace the one she was framed for slaying was not only affiliated with the militia, he was a silent leader. Meaning Butler would be facing a "family member" and would likely be set free, despite the crimes of which he was accused.

She eyed the stack of cash…

She heard gunfire.

Shit!

Leaving everything as it was, she got to her feet and ran for the living-room window, hoping Reece was okay.

20

WHAT AN ORGY OF CHAOS.

One minute Jon had been focused on watching what he hoped was Mara's silhouette against the backlit curtains in the cabin, the next all hell had broken loose.

Another guard had come up, this time from the opposite direction, so that he literally tripped over his two unconscious comrades.

Jon had no choice but to shoot.

And the moment he did, shadows emerged from everywhere. The single shot had reverberated through the forest walls like a call to war. Trigger happy, armed to the teeth, bloodthirsty shadows that lived and breathed for this shit.

Damn it, Mara. Where are you?

It was only a matter of time before his enemy combatants figured out two things—first, Butler's cabin was the target, and second, his location from where he was shooting.

He dropped to the ground and reached for his radio.

"Mara! Get out! Now!"

He dropped the radio and took out two enemy targets charging the front of the cabin. He was so focused on protecting it, he nearly missed the other one coming up behind him. He rolled over and took him out at the same time the other guy fired. Dirt kicked up next to his arm where the bullet missed him by inches, spraying his face and covering the protective goggles he wore.

They were little more than stationary targets....

His heartbeat thundered over the nonstop flurry of bullets around him and his breathing was ragged though he hadn't moved more than a few feet. But his mind wasn't on the danger to himself, it was on Mara. Had she gained access to the cabin? Had it been her shadow he'd seen? Or was she still stuck outside, desperately trying to find a way in?

He stared at his silent radio.

He easily took out another man approaching the cabin. It was easy because taking out enemy combatants was his only mission. While Mara had an agenda that would distract her from other things. That's why she needed him to provide backup.

Backup.

Damn it, he'd never truly believed he'd needed it.

In his head, he heard Darius Folsom, the Lazarus partner who had handed him this job. His words were as clear as if he was saying them next to him: "Backup is here if you need it."

Jon's silent response was that he wouldn't.

He should have known he'd live to eat those words.

If something happened to Mara as a result of his stubbornness...

His heart beat harder.

Of course, contacting Lazarus for help now was out of the question. While he understood they had extensive contacts, he couldn't trust that they'd get there in time.

But he knew of others who could.

He had no choice. There was more than himself at risk here. He had to do it.

For Mara.

He reached for his cell phone and inserted the battery, dialing the number he'd entered after he'd received it.

He spoke quietly but insistently. And was told help would arrive soon.

Ten minutes dragged by like an hour with no sight and no word from Mara, no sign of the barrage letting up and no alert that the backup he'd been promised was coming. He was running low on ammo and, damn it, they just seemed to keep coming.

The whoop-whoop of a helicopter sounded from above.

He knew a moment of relief so profound he nearly cheered.

The cavalry was here.

Or, rather, the FBI.

He'd never seen himself turning to them. And if he'd been alone, he never would have. But he wasn't alone and he had. At the very least, they could create a diversion so he could get Mara and hightail it the hell out of there.

Ironic that he'd called in the very people he had been avoiding?

Your enemy's enemy is your friend....

Of course, now he had to get Mara out of there before they could take her in.

He grabbed the last of his loaded shotguns and went mobile, tracing a wide arc around to the side of the cabin. He hoped against hope that she was holed up somewhere there, holding her own.

"Reece!"

He looked to his right to see Mara.

Thank God...

He realized she was trying to alert him to a presence to his left. He looked in time to see a bullet take a militia member out: Mara's.

"Let's go, go, go!" she said.

Running nearly back to back and firing along the way, they headed back the way they'd come.

It was rough going, with them having to stop every few feet to better launch a counterattack. They'd been discovered and reinforcements poured in, making progress slow.

Jon felt a blow to his lower chest. Air rushed from his lungs and a painful heat spiked outward from the point of impact. He'd been shot. Looked like that vest was coming in handy.

"You still with me, Reece?" Mara shouted.

He gritted his teeth. "Still here. Let's move!"

Finally they were a few feet away from the fence when he saw the hole she'd made.

Is that what had alerted the others? Had a normal guard on his rounds come across the opening and put out the alert, bringing in more than usual guards sniffing around Butler's place?

He sprayed the area and Mara ran through the exit, covering him so he could get through.

"Reece!" she shouted when he stopped. "What are you doing? We need to get out of here. Now!"

He reached for one item she hadn't seen him pick up at Trent's depot. He now removed the strap holding it to his inner calf, waited until the clearing filled then tossed the plastic explosive, hitting the detonation device right before it hit the ground.

The fallout would give them at least a five-minute lead.

Then they only had to worry about the FBI....

REECE RUSHED TO THE DRIVER'S door of the Blazer parked a mile up the road and Mara didn't fight him. She couldn't see well in the dark, but for all intents and purposes, no one appeared close on their heels. Reece's explosive had mangled the fence, complicating the others' exit. She climbed into the passenger's side and secured herself in as the Blazer spit up the ground around them. Rather than head for the road they'd come in on, he headed east on the desert floor instead, a danger when it was broad daylight. In the dark of night…

She stared as a cloud budged from in front of the full moon, seeming to illuminate their way, then she turned to keep an eye on the ground behind them.

So far so good.

They drove in silence for a good long while. Ten minutes later, Reece pulled onto a road that ran parallel to the one he didn't take. He headed south.

"Wow," she said, her heart just beginning to stop thrashing against her rib cage.

Reece took a deep breath and ran a hand over his face. "You can say that again. But we're not out of the woods yet. Not by a long shot."

"I know."

Her hand kept going to her left upper thigh.

"You're hit," Reece said.

"What?"

She looked down then lifted her hand to find it coated in blood. She'd felt a stinging sensation but had assumed she'd caught a branch or something back at the compound.

"Just a flesh wound," she said.

She was sure that was all it was. If it had been a bullet, she'd have known it.

She tore off a few inches from the bottom of her T-shirt and tied the fabric above the wound tightly to stanch the flow of blood. Then trained her eye on the back window.

Only, it appeared it was the front one she should have been watching.

"Damn." She heard Reece's low rumble.

She turned to see a familiar pickup truck approaching them in the opposite direction. She saw it pass... then hit the brakes, nearly sending the car behind it crashing into its backside.

Inside were the two militia members that had opened fire at the Winslow sheriff's office.

"What are the odds?" she asked as Reece floored it.

"About a million to one. They must have gotten word and been heading back to the compound."

"Yeah, and they caught us just as we were pulling out onto the road."

"That means the Blazer's been made."

He shut off the lights and hung a right at the next crossroads, accelerating to a speed above ninety. He shut off the air conditioner, opened the windows and went faster yet.

They were out in the middle of nowhere where roads were few and places to hide even fewer.

"I've got something to tell you," he said over the roar of the engine.

Mara peeled her gaze away from where the pickup had just turned after them.

"To get us out of that tight spot back there I called in the FBI, to create a distraction."

She stared at him as if he'd gone nuts.

"So the two goons on our tail..."

He glanced at her. "Aren't the only ones."

Hell.

She'd wondered where the helicopter had come from. She'd worried the group had experienced a healthy influx of cash from a wealthy donor; Lord knew there were enough of them.

Instead, it had been the FBI.

The very people who wanted to see her stand trial for a crime she didn't commit.

She felt for the bag tied to her gun belt.

"Did you get it?" Reece asked.

"Yeah. Now let's see if I'm going to get a chance to use it...."

21

JON HATED THE LOOK on Mara's face. He hated that what he'd said had put it there. And he hated that despite what they'd gone through—and were still facing—she was at risk.

He glanced at her bloodstained pants leg, his stomach wrenching at the thought of her being hurt: both physically and emotionally.

And knowing what he'd done may have very well caused more pain than the bullet that had grazed her.

The SUV coughed, bringing him back to the here and now. He fought to focus on the issue at hand. It was vastly important he get this right. The rest, well, the rest he'd have to work out on the other side.

If they emerged from the other side…

While the road ahead of them was currently clear, there were no guarantees it would stay that way. Unlike him, he had the feeling the two goons knew how to call for backup. And it wasn't outside the realm of possibility that he'd eventually blink to find someone in front of him as well as behind.

Possibly sooner rather than later. Which meant he had to figure a way out of this now.

He stared into the rearview mirror. He didn't know what the pickup on their tail had under the hood, but it at least matched what the Blazer had. He wasn't going to outrun these guys. Not out here, where turn-offs were few and open roads many.

There never seemed to be a big city around when you needed one....

He reached into the backseat where he'd dumped his weapons and handed Mara a sawed-off shotgun, indicating she load it. The SUV bounced over a rut in the road and he automatically reached over to brace her. She ignored him, emptying out the spent shells and loading fresh, then handed it to him.

"Load the other one back there, too."

She nodded and put the gun aside, doing as he asked.

She handed it to him. He took it. Then handed her the other one. She looked at him.

"Hold on," he said.

He slammed down on the brakes, sending the Blazer into a half-spin until they were facing the pickup. But he didn't stop there. As soon as they'd done a complete one-eighty, he stepped on the gas, evening the SUV out...and challenging their opponents to a game of chicken.

An armed one...

Jon maneuvered his shotgun out the open window, leaning the shortened barrel against the sideview mirror.

Mara did the same through the passenger's window.

They were coming up on the pickup fast. The roar of the engine was loud in his ears.

A hundred yards...

Seventy-five...

Fifty...

Thirty...

Mara shot first, her spray hitting the pickup's front grill and tires. Steam hissed from multiple holes in the radiator and the truck swerved slightly to the left before the driver righted it. Jon realized it was because she'd caught the tire. Rubber exploded from the rim like a colony of bats.

But the pickup kept coming.

Twenty...

He aimed for the windshield and squeezed the trigger.

The glass exploded.

Still the pickup came...

Jon veered slightly right while the pickup veered left, the driver shooting as they passed, taking out the back windows.

He stood on the brakes, bringing the Blazer around again, only this time he slammed it into Park, climbed out and rounded the back, using the vehicle as cover as Mara did the same on the other side.

Only one of the men got out of the pickup—the

driver. Jon squinted, the truck's interior light revealing the passenger either unconscious or out of the game altogether.

Still, the goon kept coming, walking without cover.

Jon shot…and the blast covered the lower half of the man's body. He jerked and stumbled, dropping to one knee. Then he slowly got back to his feet and continued coming.

No way…

Jon deduced he must be wearing full body armor. A new, lightweight variety he'd heard about but had never seen…until now. It had to be. No one could take a direct blast like that and still get up and walk.

"Head," Mara shouted.

Jon nodded. His head was the only unprotected part of him.

As the man walked, he shot. And the closer he got, the more accurate.

Jon squinted down the shotgun barrel, focusing on his head.

"Got it," Mara said on the other side of the Blazer.

He looked to find she had exchanged her shotgun for the vintage 1873 Winchester rifle, doing the same thing he had moments before by closing her left eye and targeting their adversary with her right.

A single bullet rent the night in two in a bright display of white gunpowder…

And the man went down.

Permanently…

MARA SAT QUIETLY in the passenger's seat as Reece drove. The Blazer resembled a piece of metal Swiss cheese. It was a miracle it was running at all. But it was.

The farther away from the site they moved, the harder her throat tightened.

"We stick out like a middle finger," Reece said.

She watched as he took his cell phone out and put in the battery while he drove. She wanted to ask who he was calling, but didn't have the energy. Did it matter?

She couldn't believe he'd called in the FBI.

"Steve? Hi, big brother. It's Jon."

She recalled him naming his siblings and Steve had been one of his older brothers. The oldest? She couldn't remember.

She wanted to tell him the FBI had probably already picked up on the signal and were likely on their way to their location now.

But why bother?

"I've got a favor to ask," Reece said. "I need you to meet me at that place we went when we were kids. The one where that Johnson kid got fresh with Jenna and we had to teach him a lesson. In twenty minutes, okay? Leave your cell phone at home."

Mara listened with half an ear, the fact that he hadn't named a location that could be followed or that he popped the battery back out of the cell mattering to her not at all.

They drove in silence for miles. He was avoiding main roads. It was a good thing, since they'd likely be discovered the instant he hit a main highway, given the condition the Blazer was in.

"You okay?" His voice broke her out of her reverie.

She looked at him, but curiously, her voice seemed to have left.

"He didn't hit you, did he?"

She lethargically shook her head. No, she hadn't been hit.

She wasn't entirely clear why she felt the way she did. She experienced the same apathy she had when he'd told her he didn't care whether she'd committed the crime or not.

He'd called the FBI....

So? a small voice inside her head said. The diversion the Feds had created was what had allowed them to escape the compound.

Still...

Minutes later, Reece pulled to a stop outside an old high school football stadium. It was late and he'd come into town through back streets. While she was sure the drivers of the few cars they'd passed had done a double take, she was relatively sure none of them did anything besides stare.

He pulled around back near the far end of the bleachers in the empty parking lot. Empty except for a newer yellow Volkswagen bug.

She watched as the driver got out. He looked so much like Reece, they could have been twins.

Reece put the Blazer in Park and got out.

"Where's your truck?" Reece asked as he gave his brother a bear hug.

The obvious closeness of the two reminded Mara of her own younger siblings and she knew a pang of sadness. Would she ever see them again?

"Samantha blocked it in the driveway with her car," Steve said. "What in the hell happened to you?"

She listened with half an ear as Reece explained that he needed to borrow the bug, and he'd recommend his brother call his wife to pick him up rather than take the Blazer back to his place.

"Damn it, Jonny, what kind of trouble are you in?"

"I'll explain later."

Steve tossed him the keys to the car and Reece thanked him. Then he indicated Mara join him.

She climbed out of the SUV, taking nothing but the bag, Reece's duffel and the Winchester with her.

"Don't call Samantha until we're gone for at least five minutes, okay?" Reece said to his brother after a brief introduction.

"Right. I'll just sit on the bleachers a bit. Sweat. Relive old memories."

Mara put one of Reece's T-shirts on the passenger seat first, to avoid any staining from her still-bloody thigh, then got in the car.

The two brothers hugged again.

"Thank you, Steve. I owe you one."

"Last I looked, you owed me about a fifty. But who's counting?"

Reece chuckled then got into the driver's side.

"Call if you need anything," Steve said.

As they drove out of the parking lot, leaving Reece's brother behind him, the new-car smell making Mara slightly nauseous, she couldn't help thinking that this was it. This was where she and Reece needed to part ways.

And just as soon as she could force her head around that fact, she'd find a way to do it....

22

Jon tossed his duffel to the king-size bed in a motel room just outside Phoenix. The place was slightly better than the last one they'd stayed in, but that wasn't saying much.

Still, everything was a bit newer and it didn't smell like stale smoke.

He watched as Mara passed him on the way to the bathroom then closed the door behind her without making eye contact.

He grimaced and sank down on the edge of the bed. They'd stripped off their gear some miles back and dumped it in a supermarket trash bin, but he lifted his T-shirt now to get a look at the impact site from the bullet he'd taken at the compound. A black circle about the size of a dime was the center of a chest-wide violent purple bruise. He absently rubbed it and winced, wishing he could get a closer look at Mara's wound.

Mara...

She'd barely spoken to him since he'd told her he'd

called in the FBI for backup, and had looked at him even less.

He could only guess what was going through her mind. In fact, he was surprised she hadn't told him to stop somewhere and let her off.

And if she had?

He ran his hands over his hair.

The bathroom door opened to reveal pretty much the same picture he'd seen the night before—hell, had it really been only twenty-four hours ago? She was wet from a shower and wore nothing but a towel. Only now her hair was short and blond, there was gauze taped to her outer left thigh and the light seemed to have left her eyes.

He questioned whether it was wise to leave her alone, but he needed a shower. He took a fresh T-shirt from his bag and tried to hand it to her, but she ignored him as she sat on the other side of the bed, her back to him, her tattoo emerging somehow ironic now that they were in a city named Phoenix.

He took a few more things from the duffel then went to the bathroom without saying anything. If she left, she left. There was nothing he could do about it.

Somehow, he got the impression she wasn't going anywhere. At least not yet.

He stood under the shower spray for long minutes, thinking about all that had happened. And everything that still might…

He hoped some kind of plan on how to proceed

would present itself soon. Because he had no idea where they needed to go from here.

A short time later, he stepped from the bathroom to find Mara in bed, wearing his T-shirt, her back still to him, feigning sleep.

And he knew an ache so acute it eclipsed everything he'd ever known....

MARA HEARD REECE COME OUT of the bathroom. She forced herself to stop biting her bottom lip and closed her eyes. She listened as he moved around the room, switched on the TV, which was preset to a local station covering the news—heat, heat and more summer heat forecast for the region—and then turned it off again. The bed moved as he sat down on the other side.

She bit her bottom lip again. Hard.

How was it she wanted nothing more in that moment than to roll toward him and lose herself in his arms?

"Mara?"

Her heart hitched, as it always seemed to do whenever he quietly said her name.

"I know you're not sleeping."

She remained silent, unmoving.

He sat for long moments. Then, she guessed by the movement of the mattress, he stretched out next to her.

No, she didn't have to guess. Despite the size of the bed, she could feel his heat next to her, hotter than any Arizona summer day could offer up.

She swallowed hard, the sound unusually loud with nothing to compete with it.

He sighed. "Okay, then. Good night."

He shut out the light, shifted then cleared his throat.

For reasons unknown to her, Mara's eyes swam in stinging tears.

He was such a good man. Solid. And he'd certainly gone the extra mile for her.

Then why was she shutting him out?

Because she had to.

Because he deserved better than her.

The soft sound in the back of her throat served to upset her further.

She'd never cried in front of anyone before. Ever.

"Mara?" he whispered, sounding too close for comfort.

She turned her head into the pillow.

"Are you all right?"

No. She wasn't all right.

Worse, she was afraid she wasn't going to be all right ever again.

She felt his hand on her shoulder. A light touch. She stiffened.

"Shh… I'm just going to lie next to you, okay?"

She wanted to tell him no. Shrug him away. Instead, she lay there as he rolled to curve against her, his hand still on her shoulder, his breath warm against the back of her damp hair.

Then his hand moved. He smoothed it down her

arm and back up again. Then rubbed her back in slow, gentle circles.

So strong. So capable. Yet so very sweet...

His attentiveness served to further expand her weakened state. A sob ripped from her throat.

"Shhh..." he said again, drawing her against him.

Against her will, Mara found herself turning toward him so they were front to front. But she didn't look at him. Instead, she buried her face in his neck and clutched him tightly, giving herself over to the barrage of emotion battling for a way out.

He smoothed his hands down over her back and up again, then tunneled his fingers into her hair, holding her closer still.

"It's just the adrenaline crash," he said softly. "It'll pass."

His providing her with a way out, an excuse for her soggy state, only made her soggier.

How was it he was so tuned into her? How did he know just what to say and when to say it? How to touch her?

Finally, the tap seemed to run out. She found herself pressing her lips to the skin of his neck. A silent thank-you? Maybe.

But when the one kiss turned into another, and she found herself curving a leg over his, bringing the T-shirt she wore up over her hip, and her bare pelvis against his...

Her hard swallow now had nothing to do with awkwardness and everything to do with need. A fundamental, overwhelming, all-consuming need to join with him, to feel him deep inside her, to explore the powerful bond that was growing between them without thought to anything else. There was no future. No tomorrow. Only this moment.

And this moment she needed to make love to him.

JON ATTEMPTED TO STIFLE his groan when Mara pressed her bareness against his jeans zipper. He'd never had a woman fall apart so fully on him before and had never held her while she cried. He'd felt as helpless as a puppy that had wandered a little far away from its mother for the first time.

He hadn't known if he was doing the right thing by touching her and was uncertain if his holding her was bringing her comfort or making things worse. Especially when her sobs had intensified.

Was he the cause?

The idea made his stomach hurt.

But now that her tears had stopped, and she was kissing his neck…

He gave up trying to hide his reaction and groaned, holding her tight, not because she needed it…but because he did.

He slid his fingers up over her face, then down to her chin, lifting her face to his. He searched her damp eyes, relieved when she didn't try to evade his gaze but rather steadily returned it.

Something opened inside of him at the naked honesty he glimpsed in those hazel depths. No. That something had already opened. It had just expanded. As it did every time he looked at her.

He eyed her full mouth, running the pad of his thumb over her lower lip, then leaning in to kiss her.

She was so beautiful. As was how she made him feel.

Kissing her brought a sense of weightlessness. As though, if he wanted to spout wings and fly, he could. Soar high above the trees. Into a space of limitless possibility and endless pleasure.

He teased her tongue with his, savoring the taste of her, the texture.

When her fingers encircled his erection, he gasped, then he groaned as she slid her tight wetness over him, tilting her hips until he was in to the hilt.

Sweet heaven...

They lay like that for a long moment, neither of them moving beyond their continued kissing. Their bodies were joined. Jon felt his heartbeat everywhere and felt hers, too.

Then the need to move within her was too much to bear....

23

MARA FELT WONDROUSLY, gloriously alive, aware of her every organ, her every cell, every molecule of air she drew in.

Aware of Reece...

He gently rolled her so she was lying on her back, then took a condom out of his discarded back jeans pocket from the side of the bed. He slowly withdrew and she moaned in protest even though she knew he'd be back. And all too soon he had sheathed himself and was positioning the hard tip of his cock against her again.

She caught her breath, staring up into his face. He was so handsome. So kind. So hot.

He surged into her. She moved to take him in all the way, but he stopped midway and withdrew again.

A small whimper escaped her. She grasped his hips, trying to force him back inside. Instead, he leaned in and kissed her deeply, until she was breathless with want.

Then he entered her again. Slowly. Torturously.

Mara came instantly.

She was so shocked by the quickness and power of her orgasm, she stared up at him in openmouthed wonder as aftershock after aftershock rocked her entire body, leaving her helpless to do anything but ride them out.

As they finally began to subside, Reece kissed her softly...then stroked her, inside and out.

If she'd been hot before, now her temperature was off the charts. She'd never achieved this sort of bliss before. This total abandon. This incredible heat.

"I love when you come," he whispered into her ear, then surged upward into her again.

She felt him everywhere—a joy, a passion, a sense of completion so absolute she was no longer sure who she was anymore. She knew nothing outside him, outside what they were experiencing....

Reece's stroke grew slowly faster, harder...

Mara moaned, wrapping her legs around his waist even as he held her down with a hand against her lower stomach, allowing for deeper penetration.

Oh, yes...

Oh, dear Lord, yes...

"I love you."

She wasn't sure who had said the words, or if it even mattered, because in that one moment as he groaned and stiffened in orgasm, and she exploded around him yet again, the only thing that did matter was that love was present....

JON FELT DIFFERENT SOMEHOW. As if he'd ventured into a hidden grotto, bathed in miraculous waters, and re-emerged a changed man.

For a long time afterward, he lay with Mara cradled against his side, her head on his chest, caressing her back as naturally as if he'd been doing it forever. And he wanted to continue doing it forevermore.

Never had he been so moved by sex.

Mostly because it hadn't been sex he'd been having.

The instant those three words had come out of his mouth, he knew them to be true. At some point over their ordeal, he'd fallen fully, hopelessly in love with Mara Findlay. And just then, it was the most remarkable thing in the world to him.

He'd thought he'd known love. Thought he'd under-stood it. But he realized now that love wasn't some-thing to be quantified or measured. It just was.

How do you know you're in love? The age-old ques-tion teased his mind.

You just know.

He got that now.

Grasped it 100 percent.

He knew beyond a shadow of a doubt that what he felt for Mara was love.

And he also knew she returned it as strongly.

"What are we going to do?"

It took Jon a moment to register her soft words. He felt them against his skin as breath before actu-ally hearing them.

"About?" he asked.

She swallowed thickly. "About ending this…."

Even though he knew she was referring to the price on her head, he couldn't help giving a start at her choice of words.

"I don't know," he admitted.

She shifted slightly, then sighed against him again.

"I think it's time we called in our backup…." he said quietly.

Her instant stiffening told him she knew exactly to whom he was referring: the FBI.

"Not now. Not this minute," he said. "Not until you're ready."

Only, he was afraid she'd never be ready.

"They'll arrest me," she said.

He didn't respond immediately.

"You know that."

"Maybe."

She shifted again, this time to move away from him.

He felt her absence so fully, he nearly shivered.

He looked to find she'd rolled completely away, her bare back to him.

"I'm open to suggestions," he said quietly.

She didn't say anything.

He rolled so he was facing her but wasn't touching. He rested a hand against the silken heat of her back.

"Mara?"

"I say you take what I have to them. Prove my innocence…."

His fingers hesitated against her skin. "I wish it were that easy."

She rolled back to face him. "Why isn't it?"

"Because we both know this is more complicated than that. It surpassed that watermark some time ago."

"No, it hasn't."

"Yes, Mara. It has."

He watched her bite her bottom lip.

"The Winslow sheriff's… Everything that happened while we've been on the run… The militia…"

She stared at him, waiting for something he wasn't sure he could give her.

"It's not enough to prove just your innocence. It's time you came clean."

She squinted at him and he glimpsed suspicion in her eyes. "I'm not following you.…"

He could tell by the tightening of her every muscle that she understood exactly what he was saying.

"Mara, you need to tell the authorities everything you know about your former 'family' and Butler.… Bring them down, dismantle them, for good."

"Authorities? And just what would they be the authority on, Jon? Guilt or innocence? Excuse me if I don't happen to trust them enough to find their own asses, much less clear mine."

She'd called him Jon instead of Reece.

The simple act made him wince in a way it shouldn't have, but did.

"But you're not alone anymore, baby. I'm right here with you."

"And what is turning over everything I know going to accomplish?"

"It'll free you from this."

"I'm already free."

"You're wanted for murder."

"By people whose opinion doesn't matter."

"Not to you. But so long as you have people hunting you, you'll never be free."

That seemed to catch her up short.

"Look, Mara," he said, needing to convince her this was the right thing to do. "Our system may not be perfect. Hell, it's anything but. But it is our system. The only one we have. The key word being *we*."

She wasn't listening to him. He could tell. She was shutting him out.

"It'll free you from the past."

She focused on him again.

"I'll be the first to admit I have no clue what you went through when you were one of them. Or what causes that look in your eyes when you internally visit a place I cannot follow. It's almost like a part of you dies."

He remembered watching her prick her finger on the cactus at his mother's house, how alone she'd looked, how isolated, cut off not only from him, but from herself...

"If we're to have a future—"

She rolled away again. "We don't have a future."

There was no body armor that would ever be available to stop her words from penetrating his skin and doing untold damage as they spun around inside like saw blades.

He tried to speak, but it took him a minute to force the words out.

"If…you're to have a future…you've got to close the door on the past."

"Closed, bolted, boarded, forgotten."

"Is it?"

She went quiet.

Jon lay back and slid his arm across his eyes, trying to ignore his own pain and focus on hers, on what needed to be said, needed to be done.

But, damn it, all he could seem to think about was how he couldn't stand the thought of her not being a part of his life anymore.

"Mara, I…"

He what?

He swallowed past the sandy wad in his throat.

"Do you trust me?"

Nothing. Then she shifted. But she didn't turn back to him.

"I know you've trusted others and had that trust betrayed." He was reaching, he knew it. "Betrayed? Hell, they set you up for murder."

She said something he couldn't make out.

"What?"

"No fair," she whispered a little louder. "I said that wasn't fair."

No, it probably wasn't. But he didn't know how else to get his point across.

"Do you trust that I'd never hurt you?"

Silence.

"I think you do."

Her lack of a vocal response told him that she might at least be considering his words. He hoped so.

"My advice would be this. Turn yourself in. Turn the information you got at the compound over. Cooperate with…them. Come to understand it's not the past that makes us, but what we do with it."

"Betray the trust that was put in me."

"Protect yourself. And place your trust where it's safe…and truly returned."

Neither of them said anything for a long moment.

"My father always said you're only as good as your word. Take away the money, the job, the family, and you're defined by what you say…what you do. Period. There is no other value of a man or a woman," Mara whispered.

"And what do you think your father would advise you to do now?"

She didn't answer.

That was it. All he had. He didn't think there was possibly anything more he could say, anything more he could do, to try to convince her to do anything other than what she was already determined to do.

Had she heard him? *Really* heard him?

He couldn't be sure.

All he knew was that the past two days' events weighed heavily on him, his emotions for her being the heaviest. And exhaustion was creeping in.

Mara shifted. He half expected her to get up and move farther away from him. Instead, she moved nearer.

He groaned somewhere deep in his chest and drew her closer, curving her back to his front and holding tight.

If this was the last time he was going to hold her, he intended to make it count....

24

HOURS LATER, JON WOKE to the unforgiving Arizona sunlight slicing through the crack in the motel room curtains and cutting a path across his face. He blinked and covered his eyes with his arm. He didn't have to look; he already knew Mara was gone. He felt her absence as profoundly as the bruise that stretched across his chest.

Still, he looked. Her side of the bed was empty. The bathroom door was open and the Winchester was gone.

He sat up and swung his legs over the side of the bed then scrubbed his face with his hands. How in the hell had he gotten into this mess?

And worse, what did he do from here?

He picked up his watch from the bedside table and looked at the time. He knew what he needed to do. He needed to go home. Close an important door of his own and put his own life in order.

Damn. How pious he must have sounded. Mr. Fathomless Pit of Wisdom. Just last week he'd had his life all planned out.

And now?

Now he needed to go face a jury of his own making.

He got up, grabbed a shower, stowed his stuff in his duffel and then walked outside to stand in the bright morning light.

If he blinked a little too hard and felt as though he'd been in the deep depths of a tunnel for too long, only he had to know that.

Mara...

Well, he was afraid he'd very well lost any chance with her forever. Because despite everything he'd said, what he had done would probably shatter whatever trust she ever had in him.

MARA SAT IN THE MIDDLE seat of the cross-country bus next to the window, staring outside at the Arizona landscape that would soon be history. Leaving Reece that morning...

She blinked quickly, pretending it was the sun that bothered her eyes.

Leaving Reece that morning had been one of the most difficult things she'd ever done, ever, outside of attending her father's funeral.

How could she have fallen so hard, so fast?

Two days ago...

Two days ago, he hadn't even been a remote blip on her emotional radar.

Now he dominated it.

His words still rang in her ears.

Do you trust me?

She shifted in her seat, disturbing the elderly lady beside her who sat with her arms crossed over her purse dozing.

"Sorry," she murmured.

"It's all right, dear."

But it wasn't all right.

What was she doing?

She hadn't slept at all last night. And she didn't think Reece had, either. She was pretty sure he'd known when she'd gotten up, collected her things and left. But he hadn't tried to stop her.

And if he had?

She closed her eyes and pressed her forehead against the glass, feeling both the heat from the outside and the air-conditioned coolness from within.

Who could say what might have happened.

But they both knew she had to do this.

What, exactly, "this" was…well, remained to be seen.

She'd taken the first bus out, which happened to be going to New York City, with stops along the way. She planned to get off at one of those stops. Which one was still a mystery.

All she knew was that she had to work this out on her own.

She had made copies of all of the documents she'd taken from Butler's safe, only some of which she'd sent via messenger to the federal prosecutor in charge of her case before catching a cab to the bus terminal.

Until her name was cleared, she planned to stay on the run.

You'll never be free...

She scrunched her eyes shut tighter.

Get out of my head, Reece.

She would have thought that to be easier than it was proving.

It was her heart she'd anticipated a problem with.

That thought made her aware of the sharp ache in her chest, one that intensified whenever she breathed.

She couldn't remember being this broken up when she'd left Butler and the compound. She'd heard childbirth was like that: even the most difficult deliveries were mostly forgotten once a mother cradled her baby in her arms. Was love like that? Once you'd gotten over the pain, did you forget about it?

No. She knew that wasn't the case here.

Reece...

She curled her fingers into her palms, her short nails biting into her flesh.

Do you trust me?

She needed to stop this...

The passenger in front of her was looking at something outside the window, then said something to the man next to him, who got up in order to look out, as well.

Mara looked out to see that a black SUV with flashing grill lights had drawn even with the bus, motioning for it to pull over.

FBI.

Damn.

She grabbed her bag. "Excuse me," she said to the woman next to her.

Her hurting heart beating erratically, she rushed up the aisle, hoping to get out the back before the bus completely stopped.

Her foot caught on something and she went flying, smacking palms first onto the rubber mat. She looked to see she'd tripped over a baby blanket. The mother apologized and picked it up while another passenger asked if she was all right.

She scrambled to gather the things that had fallen out of her bag, only to see a cell phone.

Not just any cell phone, but Reece's.

The bottom dropped out of her stomach.

She reached for it, and saw that it was live…and that there was a small note attached to the back.

"Trust me."

In that moment, Mara knew she could never trust anyone again.

25

"I NEED YOUR HELP."

Those were Jon's first words when he'd stood in Darius Folsom's office at Lazarus the morning Mara had taken off on her own…and he'd planted his cell phone on her, guaranteeing the FBI would pick her up in no time.

While he argued he'd done it for her own protection, he knew he'd also done it for selfish reasons. But not entirely. By allowing the FBI to take direct custody of her, Lazarus lost out on the lucrative bounty.

Which made his words to Darius all the braver.

Or foolish.

"Let me get this straight," Darius had said, leaning back in his chair and crossing his arms after Jon had outlined what he needed. "You cost this company money…and now you're asking for a favor?"

As ridiculous as it seemed, Jon had found himself smiling. "Yes, I am."

Darius had rocked in his chair for a few moments, then slapped his hands on the desk. "You got it."

Now, a week later, he received the call that the charges against Mara had been dropped and she'd been set free, thanks to Darius going to Lazarus partner Lincoln Williams, who was ex-FBI, among other things.

Truth was, Jon had always suspected the documentation he'd helped Mara get wouldn't be enough to assure her being cleared. She was right—the "authorities" couldn't be trusted entirely. They could be shortsighted…especially when they already had those sights set on a suspect.

So he'd felt motivated to do what he could on his end to make sure her innocence was established.

He rocked back on his heels where he packed up the last of his boxes at the house he once shared with Julie, taking a look around the place that had never been home.

He'd bunked with a fellow Lazarus buddy for the past seven days. Julie's meltdown had been as bad as he'd anticipated when he'd hit her with the news he was leaving. It had taken her this long to calm down enough to allow him inside to get his stuff.

He glanced up to find her standing in the doorway with her arms crossed.

She really was quite beautiful. At least physically. Looking at her, he didn't have to wonder how he'd stayed with her as long as he had. But there was no future for them. He understood that now. And he'd known that fact even before letting Mara into his heart. He'd had just to acknowledge it.

No, he hadn't told Julie about her. On some level, he supposed he should have. Maybe she could find some comfort in blaming their breakup on another woman.

But he hadn't wanted to hurt her any more than he already had.

Besides, if she was this hypercritical now, what would happen if she had a cheating ex-boyfriend to add to her list of why life was so unfair to her?

"How's Brutus?" she asked.

He had taken the dog with him last week. "Fine. He misses the backyard."

He would have said that Brutus missed her, but they both would have known it was a lie. At best, she'd merely tolerated the loveable canine.

He got to his feet and hefted the box to sit on top of the others on the front porch.

"Well," she said. "I just want to let you know my attorney is encouraging me to take you to court."

"For?"

She shrugged. "For breaking your promise to me."

Jon ran his hand over his hair, then let it hang from the back of his neck. "Julie, we weren't married."

He didn't want to point out they weren't even engaged.

"Not yet. But when we moved in together, that was the expectation. At least it was mine."

He sighed and shook his head. "Do what you need to," he said. Then he met her gaze earnestly. "But I recommend you not go that route. Move on, Julie. Find the man who is going to make you stop thinking about attorneys and lawsuits and how the world is always shortchanging you. A man who will make you happy. Lord knows, I never felt like that guy."

He put his keys to the house on the kitchen table, then walked through the door, turning before closing it behind him.

"I'm sorry we didn't work out."

She looked away. If she had tears in her eyes, he couldn't tell. But he did hear her say, "Me, too."

26

IT SEEMED IMPOSSIBLE to believe it had been a month since she'd come home to find FBI agents waiting for her.

Mara lowered her welding mask and then turned up the flame, the music of The White Stripes reverberating throughout the large warehouse. She stood with her legs squared, working to meld the last section of her latest sculpture to the main body. It stood seven feet high and five feet wide and she'd finished it in record time. Normally a piece of this size took her months.

Let's just say I was possessed, she thought, mesmerized by the licking flames even as she controlled them.

Or perhaps the correct word was *obsessed.*

Thirty days…

Reece…

She turned the flame up higher.

Considering all she'd gone through during that

time, she'd think the last thing to come to mind would
be the man instrumental in so much of what had happened...good and bad.

No, bad. Mostly bad.

Her hand faltered.

Damn.

She lowered the flame and pushed back her mask,
wondering when the constant obsessing over Jonathon Reece would finally stop. She placed the torch
in its stand and reached over to lower the volume on
her portable stereo. It wasn't bad enough she woke
every morning with him on her mind, and went to
sleep at night yearning for him in ways she couldn't
even begin to count.

*You spent seven days in an FBI holding cell be-
cause of him,* she reminded herself.

Do you trust me?

"No."

She responded aloud, wiped her brow against the
sleeve of her T-shirt then reached for the soda bottle
on a stool next to her.

She didn't trust him.

She didn't trust anybody.

"What bullshit."

The truth was, everything he had said, all the advice he'd given, had ultimately been right on target.
She'd stayed in that holding cell not so much because
she'd been held there—after the first few hours, they'd
offered to let her go—but because the agent in charge
had recommended she stay on when she'd agreed to

work with them to finally dismantle the militia group that had once played such an instrumental role in her life.

It still did.

I'm sorry…

She stood stock-still, letting the words echo through her.

Those two words had been waiting for her on her answering machine when she'd returned to her apartment. The message hadn't been from Reece. No. Rather, Gerald Butler had been the one to leave it.

And they weren't the only words he'd said.

She slowly sipped her soda, remembering, word for word.

I just wanted to tell you I'm sorry, Mara, he'd said. *For hurting you back then, and for setting you up to take the fall now so I could save my own ass. Out of everyone in my life, your ideals were the ones that most closely matched those I proclaimed to uphold. Ironic, isn't it? I was supposed to be the teacher. But when it came to you, well, I was the student. You deserved— deserve—better than what I've done to you. Both back then and now. The only thing that brings me comfort is I know you'll be cleared. How could you not? You've done nothing wrong. I just wanted to tell you to do what you need to. Protect yourself. And that nobody in the group will ever try to harm you again.*

"Hey, Mar?"

The live words sounded above the ones reverberating through her mind.

She looked up to see Trent standing at the top of the stairs leading to her apartment. He was part of the group she'd decided to take with her.

Thankfully, that had been all she'd heard from Gerald. And, surprisingly, they'd been words she'd needed to hear.

"Lunch in five," Trent said.

She gave him a thumbs-up, although she wasn't anywhere near hungry.

"I thought we could discuss that online gallery idea I have a little more, too."

She smiled. "Be up in five."

"Cool."

He went back inside her apartment.

Trent was one of her few conditions when she'd decided to turn federal informant. He was not to be touched and would be immune from prosecution.

She pulled her gloves off. Only she hadn't known she had to make that particular deal. It seemed Reece had been busy before catching his plane back to Colorado. He'd driven out to the bunker and pulled Trent out of there before the FBI arrived, and had dropped him at her place, where she'd found him when she walked out of the holding facility of her own volition.

She still wasn't sure how she felt about residing with someone after having lived alone for so long. But as far as bunkmates went, Trent was easy.

Of course, she was preparing a room in the opposite corner of the warehouse for him so they wouldn't be within kicking distance of each other for much longer.

She reached to switch off the oxygen and acetylene tanks when a dog's bark brought her attention to the doors. Since the warehouse wasn't air-conditioned, she liked to encourage every spare breeze she could and had left the doors open, her recovered Camaro parked just inside. She switched off the gas then headed toward the doors to check it out.

A brown dog with huge, googly eyes and a curly tail startled her when it barked just feet away.

"Hey, buddy," she said, crouching down and putting her hands out.

He wore a black, spiked collar with tags on it.

"Come here and let's see who your owner is so we can get you back home," she said.

He came to her, pink tongue lolling out of the side of his mouth, his gait resembling that of a bowlegged bulldog.

She laughed as he licked her chin.

"First mystery solved."

Mara nearly fell backward at the sound of the familiar male voice.

Her hands froze where she petted the dog, keeping him from licking places she'd prefer to keep dry even as her gaze snagged on a pair of scuffed cowboy boots that were also all too familiar.

Reece...

She realized her hands were now trembling.

"As for the second part," he said, smiling at her cautiously, "well, I guess that depends on you."

She squinted at him, though the sun was directly overhead and not in her eyes.

"The home part."

Her heart expanded like the flame on her torch when she turned up the gas.

She turned away and walked back toward the office without saying a word.

The dog followed her.

"Brutus, here," Reece said.

Brutus. Such a big name for such a small dog. But fitting.

Of course, the dog didn't listen. He trailed on her heels.

"Brutus?" she couldn't help saying, tossing the dog a chip from a bag on her desk.

She was aware Reece had followed and stood in the doorway. "Yeah. He may be a puggle, but he likes to think himself a German shepherd."

Mara didn't want to look at him. Couldn't. She wasn't ready.

What was she talking about? She had never expected to see him again.

Yet here he was, saying things that made no sense.

She puttered around with things although she was too scattered to really be doing anything.

What was he doing there?

"What are you doing here?" she asked, finally swiveling to face him.

He visibly winced. "I wanted to come by to see how you're doing."

She raised her brows then spread her arms wide. "I'm fine. There. You've seen. No thanks to you, I might add."

Her turn to wince.

That wasn't true. She was fine mostly due to him.

Had she done things her way, tried to keep running, she wouldn't have ended up in a holding cell she could walk out of at any time. She quite possibly could be still facing life in prison if not the death penalty. And she'd still be running, forever afraid of who might catch up with her.

Instead, the right man was going to trial—Butler, who'd ordered the hit on the prosecutor—and the militia had been shut down, with the worst of them also facing trials of their own.

"I deserved that," Reece said.

"You're damn right you did," she said.

Just being this close to him again, seeing him standing before her...well, made her feel alive again.

"You also deserve this...."

She walked the few steps separating them and kissed him, her arms snaking up under his arms, hands grasping his shoulders.

She had intended it as a hungry demonstration of her ongoing need for him only; she hadn't planned on things spiraling so quickly out of control.

She moved her hands to his chest, nudging him slightly away. Not all the way, just slightly.

She needed to catch her breath. She'd forgotten how profoundly he affected her.

No, scratch that; she hadn't forgotten. She just hadn't expected to experience it ever again.

Reece smiled down at her. "I think I like that better than the other."

Against her will, she smiled back.

He nodded over his shoulder. "That wouldn't happen to be me, would it?"

She looked toward the seven-foot sculpture holding the Winchester in a mixture of reverence and awe.

"Nope. It's Trent," she lied.

Reece laughed and she laughed with him.

As if hearing his name, Trent yelled down from the top of the staircase, "It's getting cold. You coming or what? Oh, hey, Reece."

Mara rolled her eyes at how casually the kid greeted him, as if he saw him every day.

"Hey, yourself, kid. Got enough for three?"

"Sure do. Come on up."

Brutus had started to bark the instant Trent opened the apartment door.

"Got enough for your little friend there, too. Here doggy, doggy, doggy."

Brutus ran up the stairs and a moment later the apartment door closed again.

Reece looked down at her, his gaze touching her as hotly as his hands.

"How long before he comes again?"

She curved against him. "Does it matter?"

"Right now? Nope."

And he kissed her....

* * * * *

REQUEST YOUR FREE BOOKS!
2 FREE NOVELS PLUS 2 FREE GIFTS!

Harlequin *Blaze*

red-hot reads!

Enjoy this sneak peek of USA TODAY *bestselling author*
Maureen Child's newest title
UP CLOSE AND PERSONAL

Available September 2012 from Harlequin® Desire!

"**L**aura, I know you're in there!"

Ronan Connolly pounded on the bright blue front door, then paused to listen. Not a sound from inside the house, though he knew too well that Laura was in there. Hell, he could practically *feel* her standing just on the other side of the damned door.

He glanced at her car parked alongside the house, then glared again at the still-closed front door.

"You won't convince me you're not at home. Your car is parked in the street, Laura."

Her voice came then, muffled but clear. "It's a driveway in America, Ronan. You're not in Ireland, remember?"

"More's the pity." He scrubbed one hand across his face and rolled his eyes in frustration. If they were in Ireland right now, he'd have half the village of Dunley on his side and he'd bloody well get her to open the door.

"I heard that," she said.

Grinding his teeth together, he counted to ten. Then did it a second time. "Whatever the hell you want to call it, Laura, your car is *here* and so are you. Why not open the door and we can talk this out. Together. In private."

"I've got nothing to say to you."

He laughed shortly. That would be a first indeed, he told himself. A more opinionated woman he had never met. He had to admit, he had enjoyed verbally sparring with her. He admired a quick mind and a sharp tongue. He'd admired her even more once he'd gotten her into his bed.

He glanced down at the dozen red roses he held clutched in his right hand and called himself a damned fool for thinking this woman would be swayed by pretty flowers and a smooth speech. Hell, she hadn't even *seen* the flowers yet. At this rate, she never would.

Huffing out an impatient breath, he lowered his voice. "You know why I'm here. Let's get it done and have it over then."

There was a moment's pause, as if she were thinking about what he'd said. Then she spoke up again. "You can't have him."

"What?"

"You heard me."

Ronan narrowed his gaze fiercely on the door as if he could see through the panel to the woman beyond. "Aye, I heard you. Though, I don't believe it. I've come for what's mine, Laura, and I'm not leaving until I have it."

Will Ronan get what he's come for?

Find out in Maureen Child's new title
UP CLOSE AND PERSONAL

Available September 2012 from Harlequin® Desire!

SADDLE UP AND READ 'EM!

Look for this Stetson flash on all Western books this summer!

Pick up a cowboy book
by some of your favorite authors:

Vicki Lewis Thompson

B.J. Daniels

Patricia Thayer

Cathy McDavid

And many more...

Available wherever books are sold.

www.Harlequin.com/Western